IF NOT US

MARK SMITH

TEXT PUBLISHING MELBOURNE AUSTRALIA

textpublishing.com.au

The Text Publishing Company
Level 6, Royal Bank Chambers, 287 Collins Street,
Melbourne Victoria 3000, Australia

Copyright © Mark Smith, 2021

The moral right of Mark Smith to be identified as the author of this work has been asserted.

All rights reserved. Without limiting the rights under copyright above, no part of this publication shall be reproduced, stored in or introduced into a retrieval system, or transmitted in any form or by any means (electronic, mechanical, photocopying, recording or otherwise), without the prior permission of both the copyright owner and the publisher of this book.

Published by The Text Publishing Company, 2021

Cover design by Design by Committee
Cover images by Shutterstock and Bigstock
Page design by Text
Typeset in Sabon 11.5/18.5pt by J&M Typesetting

Printed and bound in Australia by Griffin Press, part of Ovato, an accredited ISO/NZS 14001:2004 Environmental Management System printer.

ISBN: 9781922330796 (paperback)
ISBN: 9781922459251 (ebook)

A catalogue record for this book is available from the National Library of Australia.

 This book is printed on paper certified against the Forest Stewardship Council® Standards. Griffin Press holds FSC chain-of-custody certification SGSHK-COC-005088. FSC promotes environmentally responsible, socially beneficial and economically viable management of the world's forests.

paced action and characters we really care about.' **Tristan Bancks**

'Packed with heart-thumping, adrenaline-pumping, nail-biting action. I couldn't put it down.' **Fleur Ferris**

'A rip-roaring story—gripping and compelling. Mark Smith creates a dangerous, lawless new world and manages to champion the decency of youth. Very timely. And what makes it so powerful is that it's frighteningly believable.' **Robert Newton**

'A riveting story of survival that questions the prices of freedom and safety as well as the value of an individual life... A breakout new series full of romance, danger, and a surprisingly engaging world.' **Kirkus, starred review**

'Tense and atmospheric...Mark Smith's debut is assured, gripping and leaves you wanting more.' **Best Books for Younger Readers 2016, Sydney Morning Herald**

'A page-turner told in an unaffected, Australian voice.' **Australian**

'*Land of Fences* is an exhilarating conclusion to a massively entertaining series.' **Age**

'A shockingly good dystopian story, it has warnings of what will happen when societies become xenophobic, insular and inward looking.' **ReadPlus**

'One of the triumphs of *Land of Fences* is Mark Smith's ability to keep his readers engaged and on edge, always wondering what will happen next...[which] is balanced through Smith's intricate portrayal of love, friendship and moral courage.' **Idiom**

'An unmissable series.' **Sydney Morning Herald**

ALSO BY MARK SMITH

The Road to Winter
Wilder Country
Land of Fences

Mark Smith lives, works and surfs on Victoria's Surf Coast. The first book in his acclaimed *The Winter Trilogy*, *The Road to Winter*, is widely taught in secondary schools and loved by readers of all ages. *Wilder Country*, the second book of the trilogy, won the 2018 Indie Book of the Year for Young Adults.

For June Monica Smith—for imbuing a love of books in this most reluctant of readers

'If not us, who? If not now, when?'
John F. Kennedy

'You are failing us. But young people are starting to understand your betrayal. The eyes of all future generations are upon you. And if you choose to fail us, I say: We will never forgive you. We will not let you get away with this. Right here, right now is where we draw the line. The world is waking up. And change is coming, whether you like it or not.'
Greta Thunberg (UN Climate Action Summit, 2019)

1

Hesse slipped his board into the rack on the side of his bike and swept down the Russell Street hill. If he was lucky he'd get an hour in the water before dark. May was the best month for waves, with gentle offshore breezes and in-between-sized swells, like the whole coast was drawing breath before the arrival of winter. He loved this feeling of flying down the hill, with the promise of waves ahead of him and his weekend homework buried in his backpack in his bedroom.

School was done for the week and the next two days he'd be tied up working in the surf shop. That didn't worry him, though—the water was crowded on weekends with surfers from the city. But Friday arvos were golden: just the local crew, the tradies finishing early and the schoolkids racing each other from the bus stop to the beach.

He reached the corner and swung left onto Ocean Road, past the general store with its two petrol bowsers standing out front like sentries, and on to the surf shop. It was a converted mechanic's workshop, a big barn of a place that Theo Turnbull had been running forever.

Hesse mounted the kerb and skidded to a halt in the gravel car park. Theo was in the shaping bay, one hand holding a worn piece of sandpaper, the other caressing the rail of a foam blank he was working on. Most boards were factory-made these days, but Theo still shaped his own for special customers.

'Hesse, my main man,' he said, looking up. 'You're in a hurry.'

He always spoke like that—like the seventies had never ended and *Morning of the Earth* was still showing at the Shelbourne hall.

'Need some wax,' Hesse replied. 'You should finish early and come for a surf. It's small but Haystacks should be okay.'

'And every tradie on the coast will be crowded onto the one bank, yahooing and carrying on like it's New Year's Eve.'

Hesse looked at Theo. His hair was still thick and his ponytail long even though he was pushing sixty. When he was shaping like this, he tied his beard into a strange sort of bun and tucked it inside his T-shirt. The fine dust from the foam blank sat in the creases of his face making him look like some sort of nightmarish snowman.

'You need to be careful. You'll frighten the customers away,' Hesse said.

Theo smiled, showing the gap between his front teeth. 'Wax, you say? You know where it is. That'll be on the account, will it?'

Theo had taken Hesse under his wing when Hesse's father had died seven years ago. Trevor Templeton paddled out at Razors one bleak winter's afternoon and never came back. No body. No board. Nothing. It was like he'd been swallowed by the ocean. Theo was meant to surf with him that day, but he'd been held up at the shop. By the time he'd driven out to the point, it was almost dark and low cloud had rolled in. Razors broke half a kilometre out to sea. Theo had waited for his friend to return to shore but Trevor never arrived. The weather had turned that night; the offshore shifted to a vicious southerly gale. By the time they'd got a boat out, Trevor would have been in the water for five hours. They'd searched through the night, risking their own lives in the conditions, but found nothing.

It takes longer than seven years to get over something like that, but Theo had helped Hesse through the worst of the pain.

'See ya tomorrow,' Hesse said, grabbing a block of Mrs Palmers off the shelf behind the counter.

'Don't be late. It's going to be a sunny weekend. We'll be flat out.'

Hesse gave him the upward nod that ended most of their conversations. He tucked the wax into the crate attached to the carrier, sliding it under his wetsuit and towel.

He rode around the side of the surf shop, cut through the Rotary playground and rejoined Ocean Road in front of the surf lifesaving club. From there he braced for the climb up the hill towards the lookout. As he emerged from the protection of the trees, the offshore hit him and he instinctively turned seaward. Haystacks was a kilometre further along the coast but he could tell by the way the sets were hitting the end of Wangim Point that he'd be in for a good surf.

Reaching the top, he swung off the road, riding the dirt track like he was surfing a wave, banking on the corners and shifting his weight in the seat.

The car park at Haystacks was only half full—a good sign. Hesse stashed his bike in the tea trees, changed quickly into his wetsuit and ran down the track onto the open beach. There were a dozen surfers in the water. He hoped Jago Crothers wasn't one of them. Jago was a couple of years older than Hesse. He was apprenticed to his dad, Bob, Shelbourne's only motor mechanic. For reasons Hesse could only guess at, Jago seemed to enjoy nothing more than hassling him whenever they found themselves surfing the same break. It wasn't as though Hesse had ever done anything to aggravate him, not that he could remember, anyway. And everyone else seemed to like Jago, with his Ryan Gosling smile and smooth manner.

Hesse hadn't seen his pimped-up ute in the car park, but Jago had plenty of mates who could have given him a lift.

The paddle out was easy. Once he got past the shore break, Hesse stroked towards the other surfers who were congregated on a clean right-hander. The waves always appeared a little steeper and hollower from water level, but the size was manageable. Hesse sat up on his board just wide of the pack and watched. Even with the sun in his eyes, he recognised

Steve Daly's familiar style. Quick to his feet, he was perfectly balanced as he leaned into a bottom turn, one palm almost touching the face of the wave. Hesse was on nodding terms with Steve, though they'd never spoken. It was the way with most of the older locals—a nod, maybe a brief 'g'day', then back to business.

Hesse moved into the line-up, watching the horizon for the next set. Finding your spot was tricky when you first got out. He kept an eye on the surfers around him, noting the way they paddled continuously to counter the cross-current.

He was starting to feel comfortable when he heard a familiar voice.

'What are you doin' out here dipshit?'

Hesse hadn't spotted Jago in the glare.

'Worried he'll out-surf ya, Jago?' It was Steve Daly.

This was something new: one of the older guys speaking up for Hesse.

Jago smiled. 'In what universe would that ever happen,' he replied.

A set was approaching and the pack was on the move. Hesse felt a tug on his legrope and turned to see Jago pushing past him. He dug in deeper and the two of them went stroke for stroke. Jago was strongly built, his tanned arms rippling below his short-armed wetsuit. His long, sun-bleached hair swept back off his face as he turned and glared at Hesse.

Hesse paddled over the top of the first couple of waves but spotted his chance with the third. He was the furthest inside, giving him right of way. He pivoted his board and stroked easily into the wave, feeling the familiar surge under him as he sprang to his feet. He'd gone a little deep on the peak so he was behind the spilling lip when he came out of his bottom turn. Unfazed, he found a little extra drive and flew out onto the face. Everything was in the moment then, all muscle memory and instinct. He was lining up a slap off the lip when Jago dropped in barely a metre in front of him. Hesse maintained his speed determined not to give up the wave he'd earned. Ahead of him, Jago carved at the face like it was his enemy, slashing fast turns and leaving Hesse in his wake.

Finally, just before the wave exhausted itself on the shore break, Jago cut back sharply and slammed his board into Hesse's ankles. They fell together in a tangle of arms and legs.

The punch came fast and unexpected, hitting Hesse hard on the cheekbone. He surfaced, stunned and gasping for air. Jago stood next to him in the foaming white water.

'Sorry, dipshit,' he said, all innocence. 'I didn't realise you were behind me on that one.' But the smirk on his face was a challenge.

Hesse felt his cheek. A lump was forming.

'You knew I was there,' Hesse said, trying to stand up for himself but there was a tremor in his voice.

Jago glanced back towards the other surfers then brought his face up close to Hesse's. 'What if I did? What are you gunna do about it?'

He laughed when Hesse didn't respond. 'Yeah, I thought so,' he said, giving Hesse a shove. 'Now why don't you crawl back to main beach and surf with the other grommets.'

Jago slid onto his board and paddled out again.

Hesse staggered up the beach and sat down. He should go straight back out and let Jago know he wouldn't be intimidated, but he didn't want a fight. He looked along the beach to see if there was another peak he could surf. There was nothing as good, but he decided on a left-hander a hundred metres back towards town.

Hesse surfed on his own for another hour. By the time he made his way off the beach it was almost dark. The cool evening air bit at his skin as he peeled the wetsuit off and struggled back into his clothes. His head throbbed. He could feel the swelling below his left eye and it was starting to make things blurry. With his gear packed into the crate and his board in the rack, he wheeled his bike out of the tea trees. The car park was deserted now but he saw a girl sitting on the rail of the platform, directly beneath the only light. She was hunched against the breeze, a mass of black curls spilling from the hoodie she'd pulled over her head. The glow of the light framed her against the gathering darkness.

Hesse couldn't see a car or another bike. She must have been on her own. It'd take her half an hour to walk back to town. He knew all of the kids in Shelbourne and she wasn't familiar.

'Hey,' he said, approaching her. 'Are you okay?'

The girl ignored him. She stared out to sea.

Hesse was in two minds. If he was any later getting home his mum would worry, but he didn't feel good leaving the girl there. He put his bike down.

'Hey,' he said again.

When she looked up the hoodie fell back a little revealing a girl about his age.

'*Hai*,' she said. She had an accent. Hesse thought maybe German.

'Are you okay?' Hesse asked again.

'You said that already.'

'Sorry. It's, um, getting late. Are you heading back to town?'

'No. I'm okay. Thank you.' She seemed to clip the end of each word.

Hesse studied her for a moment longer. 'See ya, then,' he said.

'Yes,' she said. 'I see you, too.'

'No, I mean, I'll see you later.'

'Why?'

Hesse stepped closer. 'Where are you from?' he asked.

She pointed towards town.

'Shelbourne?'

'*Ja*, of course.'

'I haven't seen you around,' he said.

'No,' she said. 'You haven't.'

'Are you waiting for someone?'

She shook her head.

Hesse felt awkward talking to girls at the best of times, and he didn't want her to feel he was hassling her. 'Well,' he said. 'I'm off then.'

'Okay,' she said.

Hesse shrugged. He picked up his bike and wheeled it to the beginning of the track. He looked at the girl one last time. She was hunched forward again and looking out to sea.

2

'What happened to you?' Imogen dropped the bag of peanuts she was holding and gently touched her son's jaw, turning his cheek to the light.

'Just an accident in the water,' Hesse said. 'Got hit by my board.'

'That's quite a lump,' Imogen said.

'It's fine. I can hardly feel it.'

'It needs ice. How did it happen?'

'I got rolled in the shore break.'

Imogen opened the freezer and took out a cold pack. 'You need to be more careful,' she said, wrapping it in a tea towel and handing it to him. She looked at him in that mother's way, trying to read the things he wasn't telling her. 'Anyway,' she added, 'you're late.'

'Yeah, sorry,' Hesse said, relieved at the change of subject. 'There was a girl at the beach. I stopped to see if she was okay.' He scooped a handful of nuts into his hand.

'Hey, they're not for you,' she said slapping his wrist. 'What do you mean? Who was she?'

'Dunno. Never seen her before.'

'How old?'

'About my age.'

'Was she waiting for someone?'

'I don't think so.'

'So, you left her there?'

'What was I going to do, Mum? Drag her onto my bike?'

Imogen looked at her watch. 'Damn! I've got people arriving in fifteen minutes.'

'Mum. I'm sure she'll be fine.'

Imogen emptied a bag of chips into a bowl then peeled the wrapper off a block of expensive-looking cheese. She sighed. 'I'll drive out there and make sure she's all right,' she said.

Hesse knew nothing he could say would dissuade her. He almost found it endearing, the way his mum carried the responsibilities of the world on her shoulders.

'What's going on? Who's the food for?' Hesse stood in front of the fridge with the door open, hoping to find something other than hummus and carrot sticks.

'I told you this morning, if you'd been listening. We've got a gathering here tonight.'

'A gathering? Is that what hippies call a meeting?'

She stuck her tongue out at him. It was a standing joke between them. The Tibetan prayer flags strung across the porch, the incense, the Indian rug on the lounge-room floor—Hesse had never known any other home, but he'd been inside his friends' houses and they weren't like his. They were all polished floorboards and flat-screen TVs.

'Shelbourne Action again?' Hesse asked. His mum had been part of the local environment group for five years.

'You know Hadron's selling up?'

Hadron owned the coalmine and power station at the top of the valley behind Shelbourne.

'Yeah, I heard.' Hesse touched the cold pack against his cheek. 'The kids on the school bus are all talking about it. A lot of their parents work at Hadron. They could lose their jobs.'

'It's not just about jobs, Hesse,' Imogen said, picking up her car keys. 'You should sit in on the meeting. You might learn something.'

'Ah, so it is a meeting!'

Imogen looked at her son. 'Yes, Mr Smartarse,' she said. 'It *is* a meeting. When did you get so cynical?'

Hesse shrugged.

Imogen was at the back door. 'If anyone arrives early, look after them, will you? And put the chips and dips on the table in the lounge room.'

'What's for dinner?' he called after her.

There was no response, just the sound of the car door closing and the Subaru's motor turning over.

'Right then,' he said to himself. 'Pasta.'

Imogen was a nurse and it usually fell to Hesse to cook dinner when she worked late shifts at the hospital in Castlereagh. He dropped the cold pack on the bench, put a pot of water on the stove to boil and started dicing an onion. It'd be his third pasta meal this week. He had zero interest in the meeting, and he had homework to do, so he'd hopefully have the pasta done before the hippies arrived. He knew who'd be coming: a couple of radical mothers whose kids went to the primary school, a few retirees with nothing better to do on a Friday night and maybe some weekenders who'd left work early to beat the traffic. And he knew who wouldn't be coming: anyone from the football club, the netball club, the surf lifesaving club, the men's shed or any of the other organisations in town that Hadron had been donating money to for decades. The company's name and logo were plastered in orange and white lettering all over Shelbourne.

As far as Hesse could tell, Shelbourne Action had pretty much nothing to show for all their market stalls and petitions about the emissions from Hadron's smokestack and the thin layer of coal dust that settled over the town every time there was a northerly wind. The government ignored them and for every letter they got published in the *West Coast Chronicle*, there were another two praising Hadron for supplying new footy jumpers or play equipment at the kindergarten.

Hesse had barely got the onion and garlic in the pan when the first knock came at the front door. He pushed the pan off the burner and walked down the hallway. There were three figures silhouetted behind the frosted glass. When he opened the door, he didn't recognise any of them—a hulk of a man in his early thirties with a full beard, a smartly dressed young woman carrying a briefcase, and a middle-aged man in a suit.

'We're here for the meeting,' the woman said, stepping closer to look at Hesse's face. 'That's quite a shiner. You should have some ice on it.'

Hesse had forgotten to look in the mirror. Maybe it was worse than it felt.

She smiled. 'Sorry, I'm a doctor. Can't help myself sometimes.'

'Come in,' Hesse said, leading them through to the lounge room. 'Mum's just ducked out. She'll be back in a tick.' He remembered the chips and dips and quickly brought them in and put them on the coffee table.

'Nice place you've got here,' the younger man said, following Hesse back into the kitchen. 'I'm James. But everyone calls me Bear,' he added. He was huge—Hesse guessed nearly two metres tall. He had to duck to get through the doorway. And the hand he offered was like a paw.

'Hesse,' he said.

'Hesse? Interesting name.'

'Yeah, some author Mum liked back in the day.' He'd been explaining his name since primary school.

The other two sat on the sofa, already deep in discussion.

'How does the other bloke look?' Bear said, pointing at Hesse's eye.

Hesse touched his face again. The bone was tender under his fingertips, and he felt like he was squinting on one side.

'Need a hand with anything?' Bear asked.

'Nah, I'm good. Just cooking some dinner.'

'No shit? I could smell the onion from the street.'

Bear watched as Hesse added chopped capsicum to the pan.

'You know those two?' Hesse asked nodding towards the couple in the lounge room.

'Nope, just met them in the front yard.'

There was another knock at the door.

'Go,' Bear said, 'I'll look after this.' He grabbed the pan and expertly flicked the handle to keep the ingredients moving.

Hesse got caught up greeting people as more and more arrived. The lounge room was suddenly looking small. There weren't enough chairs and people were forced to stand or sit on the floor. By the time he made it back to the kitchen, Bear had the pasta plated up with the smell of a tomato and basil sauce filling the room.

'I'm a chef,' Bear explained.

'Looks good,' Hesse said sitting down at the table. 'Want some?'

'Nah. I've already eaten, thanks. But you get stuck in.'

He'd only had a couple of mouthfuls when Imogen pushed through the back door. She stopped and stared at the twenty or more people crowded into their lounge room. 'Shit!' she said. 'I should have bought more dips.'

'Did you find the girl?' Hesse asked.

'Yeah. I gave her a lift home.'

'And?'

'Tell you later,' she said, dropping her keys on the bench. She pushed the concertina doors fully open between the kitchen and the lounge room and people spilled out, pulling up chairs at the table with Hesse. He recognised a few of them from around town. There were only a thousand people in Shelbourne, so you got to know most of them, by sight at least.

He finished his pasta and gave Bear a thumbs up. Then he dished up what was left in the pan and held the plate up for Imogen.

Fridge, she mouthed and pointed.

Hesse dropped his plate in the sink, put hers in the fridge and retreated to his bedroom with the icepack. He had two assignments he'd been putting off and he'd be working at the surf shop all weekend. When he checked his phone, SnapChat was alive with pictures from a party some of his classmates were at in Castlereagh. There were lots of advantages to living on the coast but sometimes it was isolating. Imogen worked rotating shifts and she was usually too tired to drive him to a party forty kilometres away, let alone give him a lift home.

Hesse put on his noise-cancelling headphones and opened his laptop. He was writing an essay on climate change for English. The more research he'd done the angrier he'd become. He wanted to feel positive about the future but the government wasn't doing much to give him hope. Their policy seemed to be to ignore it and hope it went away.

After half an hour he slipped the headphones off. He needed a hot Milo. The hubbub of conversation and raised voices hit him as he opened his bedroom door. He was surprised to see even more people had arrived. They'd filled the hallway now and he had to politely nudge his way through to get to the kitchen. Catching Imogen's gaze, he raised his eyebrows and mouthed, *Wow!* She nodded and turned her attention back to the guy who was speaking. It was the middle-aged man in the suit who'd arrived early.

'My name's Oliver Bairstow,' he said. 'I'm here because everything has changed now that Hadron has put the mine and power station on the market. I've been studying their corporate structure and looking through their annual reports. I think they want to offload their Shelbourne assets—they're old and dirty and don't fit with the company's push into renewable energy.'

'But,' Imogen interrupted, 'that just means they'll sell to another company. We'll still have the mine and the pollution.'

Oliver took his time to answer. 'I don't want to speak out of turn. I know some of you have been fighting Hadron for years, trying to hold them accountable for their emissions. But our first objective should be to block the sale, mount a campaign that exposes Shelbourne for what it is—the most toxic power station in the country. We need to put any other company off buying it.'

'Then Hadron will just keep doing what it's been doing for fifty years—digging a bigger hole and pumping out more filthy emissions,' Imogen said.

'I don't think so.' Oliver was on a roll. He sat forward on his chair, resting his elbows on his knees and intertwining his fingers. 'If they can't sell, I think they'll shut it down.'

Hesse took the Milo tin from the cupboard, but his attention was on Oliver. He sounded like he was used to public speaking. His eyes moved around the room and his words came slowly and deliberately.

'What sort of a campaign are you talking about?' Bear asked. 'No offence to anyone here, but it doesn't look as though Hadron has been bothered much by Shelbourne Action so far.'

There was some audible tut-tutting, but an equal amount of head-nodding.

'Well,' Oliver said. 'How many of you have been involved in large-scale environmental campaigns?'

'I was at the Franklin blockade,' an older woman said.

'Roxby Downs in '83,' another chimed in.

'The Iraq War rallies in the '90's. They were huge,' a man said and was met with a general murmur of approval.

'Okay,' Oliver said, trying to wrestle back control. 'They were all terrific campaigns, but really, only one of them was successful.'

'No dams, no dams!' the woman chanted, and everyone cheered.

Hesse grabbed the milk from the fridge and put a pot on the stove. He'd heard of the Franklin Dam protests. Somewhere in Tasmania.

Oliver raised his hand and waited for a bit of quiet. 'Things are very different now,' he said. 'Modern campaigns need to target two things: banks and shareholders. Coal is on the nose internationally. Investors are leaving it in droves and banks don't want their brands associated with it.'

'But how do we get to the banks?' Imogen asked.

'Social media,' Oliver said. It's like he'd rehearsed this presentation. Hesse thought he would be a good person to interview for his essay.

'We need to get as many of us on Twitter as possible. Politicians and companies monitor it closely—who's mentioning them, what's being said. The thing is, any prospective buyer needs to get their money from banks. And if banks' shareholders see their company's name getting dragged through the mud for investing in fossil fuels, they'll act.'

A few people laughed at the idea of being on Twitter.

'Can I get that on my phone?' someone asked.

'I've only just got onto Facebook.'

Hesse rolled his eyes, but his attention was pulled back to the stove as the milk boiled over. He quickly turned the gas off but the smell of burning milk filled the kitchen. Conscious of everyone watching, he tipped the remainder of the milk into his cup and smiled meekly at Imogen. He negotiated the crowded hallway again and went back to his room.

Shutting the door was a relief. His laptop glowed on the desk, his unfinished essay glaring at him from the screen. But listening to Oliver had triggered his curiosity. He'd always accepted that the mine and power station were part of Shelbourne. On still nights, the thrum of the turbines rumbled down the valley and melded with the sound of the ocean until you couldn't tell them apart. And the smokestack rising above the ridge was like an exclamation mark on Hadron's ownership of Shelbourne. Its emissions were near invisible but on certain winds their acrid smell would fill the valley and settle like a blanket over the town.

Hesse brought up a Google Earth shot of the mine. The open cut was huge, almost as big as the town. The pit was kidney shaped and came close to the houses along Ridge Road. The scar on the landscape contrasted with the green of the heathland and forest that surrounded it. He hadn't realised the river ran right through the mine site. To the north was the power station. He magnified the image but the closer he got the more blurred it became. Strange. He wondered if that was deliberate.

Next, he searched for Hadron. It was a multinational company with its headquarters in Texas, and a yearly turnover of two billion US dollars. He thought of the group of small-town activists in the next room—his mum among them—and wondered how they could ever take on a company like Hadron. This was David versus Goliath times a hundred.

Hesse disappeared down the internet rabbit hole for another hour, somehow ending up watching the last ten minutes of the 2012 AFL Grand Final. He was developing a theory that the internet had discovered a secret means of making time stop but also move faster.

When he resurfaced and took his headphones off, the noise from the meeting had abated. He ventured out to the kitchen again and found his mum talking with Bear, Oliver and the doctor who'd arrived with them. Everyone else had left. The chips bowls were empty, and the hummus dish looked like it had been licked clean.

'Hello, luv,' his mum said. 'Did you get your homework done?'

'Yeah, most of it,' he lied.

'Thanks for having us,' Bear said. 'I reckon you've really started something here tonight.'

'Oliver did all the talking,' Imogen said.

'Yeah, but someone had to get the ball rolling,' Bear persisted.

'The ball's been rolling for years,' Imogen said. 'It's just that no one seems to have noticed until now.'

The young woman held her hand out to Hesse. 'I'm Ruby,' she said. 'How's that eye feeling?'

'It's okay.'

'Keep icing it,' she said.

Ruby looked too young to be a doctor. Her blonde hair was pulled back in a tight ponytail, she had a surfer's tanned skin and wore no make-up.

They moved towards the front door in some unspoken agreement that it was time to go. Oliver and Ruby left together but Bear lingered. Imogen shot a glance at Hesse and he retreated to the kitchen, leaving them on the porch.

The smell of the crush of bodies lingered in the lounge room, though the odour of burnt milk almost overrode it. Hesse cleaned up the empty plates and heaped them on top of his pasta bowl and the pan in the sink. They'd keep till morning. He heard the front door close, his mum's shoes thrown off and the slump of her body into the couch. The springs groaned.

'Bloody hell,' she said. 'Who'd have thought so many people would be interested in trying to shut down the mine?'

'You talking to me?' Hesse called from the kitchen.

'No. I'm talking to God. Who do you reckon?'

Hesse walked through to the lounge room, lifted his mum's legs, sat down on the couch and rested her feet back on his thighs. 'You should eat,' he said. 'Do you want me to heat up the pasta?'

'No, I'm too tired.'

'Bear seems like a nice bloke,' he ventured, squeezing her toes through her rainbow socks.

'Yeah, I suppose he's all right.'

Hesse let it go.

'So, what was the story with the girl at the beach?' he asked.

'Dutch girl,' she said. 'On exchange for a term. Staying with the Turners. Not a happy camper.'

This was the way his mum spoke when she was tired—short, sharp, straight to the point.

'Why was she out there on her own?' Hesse asked.

'Who knows? She didn't say much. Barely got a word out of her.'

'The Turners don't have any kids,' he said. 'Why wouldn't they put an exchange student with a family?'

'Honestly, luv, I don't know. Anyway, she's going to Castlereagh High, so you'll be able to ask her yourself.' She swung her legs to the floor and stood up. 'I'm going to bed,' she said. 'And you've got work in the morning.'

Hesse was tired, but his brain was still ticking over. 'I heard Ruby say something about the emissions from the smokestack.'

Imogen sighed and leaned against the doorframe. 'She says there are really high rates of respiratory infection in Shelbourne. She's only been working at the clinic for twelve months, but she reckons they're way above the norm.'

'And she thinks Hadron is to blame?' Hesse asked.

'What's the one thing we've got that the other towns on the coast don't have?'

'An awesome right-hander off the point?' Hesse said.

'A coalmine and power station. That's what.' She turned her back. 'Switch off the lights when you go to bed,' she said.

'Hey,' he said.

His mum smiled. 'Fenna.'

'What?'

'The girl's name, it's Fenna.'

'How did you know I was going to ask that?'

She arched her eyebrows and closed her bedroom door.

3

Theo was already at work when Hesse arrived. It was a sunny morning and soft light filtered through the mist that hovered over the river across the road from the shop. The road was quiet for now, but it would be busy soon. It was always the same at this time of year—everyone wanted to enjoy the last of the warmth before winter. Easter used to mark the turning of the season, but now it was more like June. With the research he'd done for his essay Hesse wondered whether climate change was already having an effect.

'You been in a fight?' Theo asked as Hesse walked into the shop. His eye hadn't swollen any more overnight, but the bruising was coming to the surface. Hesse told him what had happened in the surf the previous day.

'Jago Crothers is a dickhead,' Theo said. 'His problem is he's never had to work an honest day in his life. His old man's given him everything. He thinks he can get away with anything because of his pretty-boy looks, but he's as dumb as a box of hammers.'

Hesse ran a finger over his cheekbone and winced.

'Anyway, things might change for him if Hadron shuts down,' Theo continued.

'What do you mean?'

'Bob Crothers' workshop has the contract for all of Hadron's vehicles. He's got people in Shelbourne offside by charging so much—just about everyone has their cars serviced in Castlereagh these days. So, Hadron is the only thing keeping him afloat. If they can't find a buyer and decide to shut down, he'll be out of business within a month.'

Hesse didn't want to see anyone lose their job, but the idea of Jago being forced out of town was appealing.

'Anyway,' Theo said, 'onto more important things. Coffee?'

'You've asked me that every day I've worked here, I reckon. And have I ever said yes?'

'Not yet. But the day will come when you give in to the irresistible lure of the bean.' Theo was halfway out the door, heading for the Fat Controller, the cafe just down the road. It was run by a couple of sea-changers who'd worked on the railways all their lives. 'Roll the boards out and give the front a sweep. I've set up the till,' Theo said.

Hesse liked the familiarity of these conversations—the way that he knew exactly what Theo would say. The second-hand board racks were on rollers and he wheeled them out onto the wide concrete apron at the front of the shop. Five racks in all, then the longboards to be laid one by one on the grass verge at the side of the car park.

The day passed quickly once the road started to fill. Theo had been right—they were busy with customers wanting new boards, wax, the odd wetsuit and there were always punters looking for a bargain on the second-hand racks. It was a good business day; they were regularly ringing up sales.

After lunch, Hesse watched a boy looking longingly at a new board. He knew just the right degree of interest to show when a young surfer pulled a board off the rack to feel the weight, check the thickness and shape. He gave them some time to hold it, to imagine it under their feet on an uncrowded beach break.

'Local shaper,' he said, eventually. 'Made for days like today.'

A man, probably the boy's dad, appeared from behind the rack. 'There you are,' he said. 'The second-hand ones are out the front, mate. We can't afford something like that.'

The boy carefully placed the board back on the rack and smiled sheepishly at Hesse.

'Theo's out there,' Hesse said. 'He'll fix you up.'

Hesse didn't see the Dutch girl slip into the shop, she just seemed to materialise behind him. He turned and almost bumped into her.

'*Hai*,' she said.

'Hi,' Hesse replied. He didn't know where to look. She was standing so close he could smell the shampoo in her still-damp hair. She had startling blue eyes and a spray of freckles across her nose.

'I'm Fenna,' she said, holding out her hand very formally. 'And you have a black eye.'

'An accident in the surf,' he said, dipping his head and shaking her hand. Her skin was soft against his, her fingers long. 'I'm Hesse.'

'*Haas.*'

'Close enough,' he said.

She gazed around the shop, looking for something.

'Can I help you with anything?' Hesse asked. Behind her, Theo stuck his head through the door and winked at him.

'Why is it so cold here?' she replied. She wore the same hoodie as last night, with a pair of cut-off denim shorts, black tights and sneakers. She hugged her arms to her chest.

Hesse was confused. 'In here you mean?'

'Everywhere. I thought Australia was a warm place.'

Hesse supressed a smile. 'It is. In summer.'

'I saw you surfing yesterday. Why were there no girls out there?'

Hesse was having trouble keeping up. This girl was all over the place. She sounded way too direct, but he figured English wasn't her first language. 'Um, sometimes there are.'

'Can you teach me to surf?' she asked

'Sure,' he said. 'But you'll need a wetsuit. The water's cooling down.'

'So,' she hesitated. 'They are expensive? Wetsuits?'

'We don't sell second-hand ones, if that's what you mean.

You'll want a winter suit and they start at three hundred bucks.'

Her eyes widened. '*Driehondred*?'

'Yep.' He guessed this was way out of her price range.

'Okay. Maybe I come back another time.' She turned towards the door.

'Wait,' Hesse said. He wanted her to keep talking—the halting way she spoke, the way her brow furrowed as though she was thinking carefully about the right words to use—it had all somehow made his working day seem brighter. 'My mum has an old wetsuit she doesn't wear much. I reckon she'd lend it to you.'

'Your *moeder* is Imogen?'

'The one and only.'

'She is nice. She drove me home last night.'

'She's everyone's guardian angel, my mum.'

Fenna looked confused.

'Never mind. She's got a wetsuit you can borrow.'

'Okay! Good,' she said, allowing herself a brief smile. 'Can we start today?'

Hesse shook his head. 'I've gotta work,' he said, lifting his hand and vaguely pointing at the sales desk. He had no idea why he was like this, why he lost his nerve around girls, why his sense of humour deserted him. He could joke with his mates or with Theo all day long, but when he got into a conversation with a girl it was like he was second-guessing everything he said.

'Ah, of course,' she said. 'Tomorrow?'

'Working again, sorry.' He saw the little wave of disappointment cross her face. 'But I finish at four on Sundays.'

'Okay,' she said again. 'That is good. Four o'clock at my place.'

'Excellent,' he said, realising immediately he never used that word. 'Tomorrow at four. You're staying with the Turners aren't you?'

'Ja,' she said, and disappeared out the door.

'Hey,' he called after her. 'Have you got a surfboard?'

But she was gone.

By pack-up time Hesse felt as though he'd worked two days, not one. The flow of customers hadn't let up. Theo was exhausted too but they both knew there'd be fewer days like this once winter arrived. After they'd wheeled the racks back in and stowed the longboards in the side room, Theo sat at the till with his glasses perched on the end of his nose and counted the day's takings.

'Who was that girl?' he asked. 'She seemed to know you.'

'Which one?' Hesse answered, trying to sound nonchalant.

Theo looked at Hesse over the top of his glasses.

'I hardly know her,' Hesse said. 'She's an exchange student at school.'

'What was that accent? German?'

Theo never missed anything.

Hesse told him about his encounter with Fenna at Haystacks the previous night. 'She seemed much happier today,' he added.

Theo went back to his counting. When he was done, he peeled off three fifty-dollar notes and handed them to Hesse. 'Thanks for today,' he said.

Hesse shoved the notes into his pocket. 'Can I finish a bit earlier tomorrow?' he asked.

'Something to do with that girl you hardly know?'

Hesse didn't take the bait. 'She wants a surfing lesson.'

'So, of course, you directed her to Bob Young's.' Young owned the surf school that operated on the main beach.

'She's short of cash so I thought I'd offer,' Hesse said.

'You're all heart, Hesse. Helping out a girl like that. You should start a charity.'

Hesse picked up his daypack from behind the counter and stood in front of Theo, waiting for an answer.

Theo made him wait. 'Sure,' he said, finally. 'But only because it's for such a worthy cause. Who am I to stand in the way of cross-cultural learning?'

Hesse grabbed his bike from out the back and swung onto Ocean Road. He should have gone straight home—that essay wasn't going to finish itself—but he turned down the path leading to the riverbank trail. He dodged the piles of dog shit left by weekenders walking their rescue greyhounds and overweight labradors and headed upriver. The concrete path gave way to hardened dirt beyond the BMX track, then wound its way through the mimosa scrub and scraggly messmates. Every time he turned a corner the smokestack from the power station loomed larger over the landscape.

Ten minutes later he emerged onto a wide gravel road that led up to the ridge behind town. Here a three-metre-high fence topped with coiled wire crossed the river. A thick steel grate held back debris from recent rains.

Further up the hill the scrub began to thin, and he got his first glimpses of the open-cut mine. He dropped his bike and scrambled up a small embankment. What had looked like a scar on the landscape on Google Earth, was more of an open wound. The pit must have been a kilometre long, and maybe half a kilometre wide. He could see the layers of earth cut away on the sides, the lighter browns giving way to the dark brown of the coal deeper in the massive hole. An excavator with rotating buckets on an extended arm worked away at the coalface. He watched a truck wind its way down the switchback road to the bottom, where a massive loader waited. Hesse traced the road back to the power station beneath the smokestack. Another truck was emptying its contents onto a conveyor belt that fed into the mouth of the heaving, chugging beast. Even from this distance it looked old, a relic from last century, all dun-coloured metal and rusted pipes. The treeless area around the plant was shrouded in steam from the three massive cooling towers and, above it all, thin smoke drifted from the stack.

Hesse pulled his phone from his backpack and took some photos, thinking he could include them in his English assignment. He was scrolling through the pics when he heard the roar of a car engine making its way up the road. It was moving fast. A white ute with a flashing orange light on top crested the hill and pulled to a halt in a cloud of dust. A large man, bearded and wearing a high-vis shirt, hauled himself out of the cab and huffed up the embankment towards Hesse.

'G'day,' he said, not in a friendly way.

'Hey,' Hesse said, looking back towards his bike. The guy

had parked right next to it, blocking any quick escape.

'What are you up to?' the man asked. He stood a metre from Hesse, arms folded across his chest. A cap with *Hadron* on the front was pulled tight on his square head, and a nametag was stitched onto the pocket of his shirt: *Stanton*.

'Just looking,' Hesse said.

'At what?'

Hesse thought this was a pretty dumb question, given that the mine was about all you could see from up here. 'Just taking in the beauty of the landscape,' he said.

Stanton snorted. 'Smartarse, are we?'

'It's a free country.'

The man took a few seconds, looking Hesse up and down. He stared at his black eye. 'Been taking photos?' he said, pointing at the phone in Hesse's hand.

'Yeah,' Hesse said, thinking it best to take some heat out of the conversation. 'For a school project.'

Stanton nodded, clearly unconvinced. 'We've had some trouble recently,' he continued. 'Damage to the fence. Kids on bikes getting into the mine at night. You wouldn't know anything about that, would you?'

'Nope,' Hesse said. But if there were local kids riding bikes in the mine site, he had a pretty good idea who they might be.

Stanton stepped closer. There were heavy sweat stains under his armpits. 'Mind if I have a look at your photos?'

Hesse picked up the slight change in Stanton's voice. He knew he was pushing his authority.

'They're just shots of the mine,' Hesse said, shoving the

phone into his pocket.

'You won't mind me having a look then.'

'Yeah, actually, I do.' Hesse tried to hold his voice steady. 'I'm not on Hadron's land here, am I? I can do what I like.'

The man inhaled deeply, a slight curl appearing on his lip. 'I reckon you'd better piss off,' he said.

Those last two words tilted a delicate balance, and Hesse edged back towards the fence. 'Yeah, okay,' he said, avoiding eye contact now.

Stanton pulled his own phone from his shirt pocket. Before Hesse realised what he was doing, Stanton had snapped a photo of him. 'Gotcha,' he said. 'Now, if there's any more damage done up here, we'll show this to the cops.' He tapped the phone with his index finger.

'I'm just—'

'Yeah, I know. A school project. Sounds like bullshit to me. We know what's going on in town. Know about the meeting last night. Bunch of hippies and blowhards thinking they can block the sale, put us out of work. Well, I can tell you, it's not going to happen. The mine's here to stay.'

Hesse wondered if the company had a spy at the meeting.

'Now, get moving,' Stanton said, turning his back and marching to the ute. He stepped sideways to make sure he stood on the bike wheel before he wedged himself into the ute. He revved the engine and spun the steering wheel into a tight U-turn, spraying gravel and dust behind him.

4

Sunday wasn't as busy at the surf shop. Theo did a reasonable trade, but by the middle of the afternoon customers had slowed to a trickle. The weather had clouded over, so a lot of people would have made an early start back to Melbourne. Hesse liked the way the town emptied out, leaving the locals to their own devices for another week.

As promised, Theo let him finish early. Hesse borrowed a beginner's board—a foamy—from the rentals section and jammed it into the rack on his bike. It was thicker than his board and didn't quite fit. He'd found Imogen's wetsuit in the back shed the night before and had given it a good hose out to get rid of any spiders. His mum was a bit shorter and wider than Fenna, but Hesse thought the wetsuit would fit.

He didn't have Fenna's number, but he knew where the Turners lived. A ripple of excitement ran through him as he cut across the pub car park and climbed the hill past the primary school. The Turners' house had a low brick fence and a crushed-rock driveway without a stone out of place. The garden was well cared for and was dotted with bushes trimmed into the shapes of animals—a swan, a crane and even a kangaroo. There was a small patch of thick lawn that Hesse compared with the weeds and bare dirt that surrounded his own place.

As he opened the gate, Julie Turner stepped from behind a row of tall roses, a pair of secateurs in her gloved hand. 'Hello, Hesse,' she said.

Julie had worked at the kindergarten for twenty years. She knew every kid in town and never forgot a name. She spoke in a sing-song voice like everybody was still four years old.

'Hi, Julie,' Hesse replied. 'Is Fenna home?' He kept the left side of his face turned away from her, hoping to avoid having to explain the black eye again.

'She's inside, but she's not feeling well. Maybe another day for that surfing lesson, hey?'

Hesse looked towards the house. A curtain moved in the front window. He was turning to leave when the door opened and Fenna walked out onto the porch. She was dressed in the same clothes as yesterday and had a bag slung over her shoulder. '*Hai*,' she said. 'You came early.' That accent again.

Julie Turner didn't seem relieved that Fenna was apparently well enough to go surfing. 'I'm not sure you should go, sweetheart. It'll be cold. How's your headache?'

'Fine,' Fenna replied, taking the steps two at a time. She grabbed Hesse's arm and pulled him down the path.

Julie walked behind them. 'What time will you be home?'

Fenna looked at Hesse and shrugged her shoulders. 'How long?'

'A couple of hours,' he said.

'And where are you surfing?' Julie's voice had lost a little of its sing-song quality. 'Main Beach would be safest.'

Hesse felt Fenna pinch his arm. He looked at her and her eyes widened. 'Sure,' he said. 'Somewhere safe.'

Fenna rolled a bike out of a small shed near the gate. It was an old racer with turned-down bars and thin tyres. Wheeling it to the road, she noticed the look on Hesse's face.

'What?' she said.

'Are you right with that?'

She tilted her head and smiled for the first time since he arrived. 'I'm Dutch. I was born on a bicycle.'

'That must have been painful for your mum.'

It took her a couple of seconds, but then she laughed. 'Ah, it's a joke? You Aussies talk so fast, sometimes I don't know.' With that, she hitched the bag onto her back and dropped the bike just far enough to swing her leg over.

Julie had followed them to the gate. 'Be careful,' she said. Hesse didn't know whether she was talking about the riding or the surfing. 'And I'll expect you back by six.'

Fenna waved and pedalled down the hill at speed.

Hesse picked up his bike, said goodbye to Julie and took off after Fenna. She was fast. She'd reached the pub before he caught her. It was awkward riding with the big foamy sitting high in the rack.

She pulled up onto the footpath and dismounted. 'Shit!' she said. 'I've only been here a week and already she drives me crazy.'

'Julie?'

Fenna nodded. 'All the time she wants to know where I'm going, who I'm with, when I will be home.'

'Why didn't they place you with a family?' Hesse asked.

She was walking her bike now, the two of them taking up the whole footpath. 'I was meant to be hosted by a family in Castlereagh but they moved house at the last minute,' she said. 'Julie and Colin are in the Rotary Club so they volunteered to have me. It's only temporary.'

'Oi! Dipshit. That eye doesn't look too good. Did you walk into a pole or something?' Jago Crothers was leaning over the balcony of the pub, a beer in his hand. He was flanked by two men wearing Hadron caps. One of them whistled at Fenna and the others laughed.

'Hey, Dutchie,' Jago called out. 'How old are you?'

'Come on,' Hesse said to Fenna. 'Let's keep moving.'

'You know your boyfriend can't surf for shit?' Jago said.

Fenna didn't appear concerned by the attention. She smiled at Jago.

'Ooh, you see that, boys? She likes me,' he said, nudging the guy on his left so his beer slopped from the glass. He walked along the balcony, keeping pace with them. 'You should come up and have a drink with us.'

Hesse went ahead on his bike and waited for Fenna to follow. She took her time, looking up at Jago as though she was considering his offer. 'Maybe another time,' she said, putting one foot on the pedal and scooting with the other.

'You know where to find us,' Jago called after her.

The laughter of the men receded as Hesse and Fenna rounded the corner and crossed the bridge. They turned onto the river path, Hesse ahead of her now, all the smart retorts he could have made to Jago whirling around in his head.

Fenna drew alongside him. 'They were just being friendly,' she said.

'Yeah, sure. You don't know Jago. First-class dickhead.'

'*Ferst-clarse* dickhead,' she said, mimicking his Australian drawl.

This made him laugh. 'Come on,' he said. 'The surf's waiting.'

He led her past the main beach. They climbed out of town then snaked through a series of sandy tracks in the tea tree scrub, finally emerging at a beach a little closer to town than Haystacks.

'Corrals,' he said. 'It doesn't pick up a lot of swell but it'll be okay for learning.'

There was a small car park with a half-fallen fence separating the end of the track from the dunes. Hesse directed her to a spot where the tea trees arched over to form a hidden alcove. A ring of blackened stones marked the remains of a campfire, and a dirty blanket hung from a low limb. 'You can get changed in here,' he said, handing her his mum's wetsuit.

'Okay.' She pulled off her windcheater, hung it on the fence and unbuttoned her cut-off shorts.

'I'll just...' Hesse said, turning away from her.

'What?' she asked.

'I'll get changed over there,' he said, pointing back to the bikes.

'Why?'

'Cos, y'know.'

She'd already dropped her shorts and was peeling the black tights off her thighs. 'Oh,' she said. 'You are embarrassed.'

'No, it's fine.'

'Don't worry, I've got my *zwemmers* on underneath.'

Hesse didn't know if he was relieved or not. She stood before him in a red, one-piece swimsuit, goosebumps on her pale skin.

'You've seen a girl in her *zwemmers* before, haven't you?'

'Yeah, course I have,' he said, trying not to stare.

She picked up the wetsuit and started to push a leg through.

'Hang on,' he said. 'Rookie mistake. The zip goes at the back.'

She turned the suit around. As she pulled it higher, he saw it was going to be a tighter fit than he thought. Fenna started laughing. It was stuck with the crotch at her knees and she waddled around like a penguin.

'Help me' she said, bunny-hopping towards him and grabbing his shoulders.

He gripped the sides of the suit and pulled it onto her hips. Her skin was cold where his fingers met it. She jumped up and down a little and finally they succeeded in getting the wetsuit up to her stomach.

'Now,' he said, 'turn around and put your arms through.'

She had wide shoulders and she struggled to get the suit over them. Eventually, he was able to zip her up.

'There,' he said. 'Now you look like a surfer, at least.'

She wiggled and stretched, trying to get used to the feel of the neoprene then waited for Hesse to change.

He was a Zen master at getting in and out of a wetsuit, tying his towel around his waist and dropping his jeans and jocks in one swift movement, before slipping into the suit. He'd had this one for a while and it was like a second skin. It took him all of ninety seconds to be kitted up and ready.

Fenna leaned against a fencepost. 'My first lesson in Australia,' she said. 'Putting on a wetsuit.'

The beach was quiet—a few people walking dogs and a family with towels spread out on the sand. Closer to the water a father and daughter kicked a soccer ball. Hesse turned along the beach in the direction of Haystacks. In the distance he could make out the black shapes of surfers on the break he'd ridden on Friday.

Fenna had stopped next to him. Her eyes were wide and her mouth open. '*Oh mijn God*, it's so beautiful!' she said. She spun in circles like a dancer, her arms spread wide.

'I'm guessing beaches in the Netherlands aren't like this?' Hesse said.

'No,' she replied. 'Nothing like this!'

'Come on,' he said. 'We don't have a lot of time.'

He positioned the board on the sand and lay on top of it. Fenna squatted in front of him, more focused now, her eyes locked on his. His dad had taught him to surf when he was five years old. He remembered his father carrying his board onto the beach, his thick arms stretching the rash vest he always wore in summer.

Hesse must have paused then, lost in the memory.

'What's wrong?' Fenna asked.

'Nothing,' he said. She was leaning in towards him. He wasn't used to this closeness, but he reckoned he could get used to it with Fenna.

He kept the instructions brief, knowing she'd be impatient to get into the water. He wanted to tell her about reading the waves, looking out for rips and bracing herself against the sweep, but for now he got her to attach the legrope, pick up the board and wade into the shallows. 'We'll start here,' he said. 'When you're learning, the white water is your friend. We won't take on the unbroken waves today.'

She looked disappointed. Learners usually were until they tried to stand up for the first time and realised how hard it was to balance. Then they were happy to be in the shallows.

Most of the lesson was taken up with Fenna slipping off the board before she'd even got to her knees. She laughed the first few times but soon tired of falling off. Again and again, he steadied her on the board and pushed her onto the waves.

'You want to take a break?' he asked after half an hour.

'No!' she said forcefully. She continued to fall but each time she got closer to standing.

'Don't stick your bum out when you get up,' he said as they waited for the next wave. 'Think about someone grabbing you by the hair and pulling you straight up. Use your knees.'

'*Jeetje*, this is hard,' she said.

'Once you stand up the first time it's like riding a bike. You'll never forget.'

She must have fallen twenty times. The beach had emptied, and the sun spread a golden light where it broke through the low clouds to the west. Hesse was freezing. He was usually fine when he was surfing but with all this standing around, the cold was eating into his bones. He was ready to call it quits. They could come back another day.

'Didn't you tell Julie you'd be home by six,' he asked the next time she waded out to him.

'No. *She* said I should be home at six. There's a difference.'

Hesse gave her one last push off. She paddled to pick up speed, then arched her back and pushed down on the board so she could slide her legs through. She wobbled, found her balance and stood up, riding the wave onto the sand. A wild scream ripped the air and she flung her arms above her head. Dragging the board by the legrope, she pushed her way out to Hesse and jumped on top of him.

'I did it! I did it! Did you see?' She was like a six-year-old, grinning from ear to ear, hugging him and pushing him under the water. Her strength surprised him.

He swam free of her and found his feet.

'I'm a surfer! I'm a surfer!' she yelled. She filled her mouth with water and spurted it at him.

'Yeah,' he said. 'You're a surfer.'

Back in the tea trees they changed quickly. Fenna's clothes

stuck to her wet bathers, and she shivered even when she was fully dressed.

'You did well,' Hesse said. 'Most people don't stand up in their first session. You've got good balance.'

'*Ja*, of course. I've been skating since I could walk.'

'You're a skateboarder?'

She laughed. 'No, *idioot*! Ice skating. Can you do it? If there's a rink somewhere I can teach you.'

He looked uncertain. 'Maybe there's one in Melbourne.' He'd welcome any opportunity to see her again, even if it meant making an *idioot* of himself.

'Have you heard of Elfstedentocht?'

'Nope. Who's he?'

'Not who, what. The eleven cities race. Two hundred kilometres on ice. It starts in my home town, Leeuwarden.'

'Have you done it?' he asked, trying to understand the stamina needed to skate two hundred kilometres.

'*Nee*! I'm only seventeen. It hasn't been held since 1997.'

'Why not?'

'The winters haven't been cold enough. All the canals, rivers and lakes have to freeze and link up before it's safe to run. When it looks like it might happen, the whole country gets excited.'

'About a skating race?'

'It's not just a skating race. The winners are legends.'

Hesse loaded up his bike as they talked, stalling for time now, wanting to keep her there with him. They headed off slowly in the semi-darkness, riding side by side where there was room, Hesse dropping behind her when the track narrowed.

Finally, they came out of the cover of the trees at the lookout and stopped. The coast swept away below them, and the Cape William lighthouse blinked its steady warning in the distance.

'You're so lucky to live here,' Fenna said.

Hesse had never given it much thought. It was just home, the only place he knew.

'Shame about that,' she said, pointing to the smokestack at the top of the valley.

'Yeah, well, that mightn't be there much longer.' He gave her a quick rundown of the campaign.

She listened carefully, her gaze swinging between the soft light of the coast and the harsh red and green beacons on top of the stack.

'We'd better get moving,' he said. 'Julie will've called Search and Rescue.'

'Where do you live?' she asked, ignoring his attempt at humour.

'Up behind the supermarket. At the top of Russell Street.' He guessed this didn't mean a lot to her, so he pointed. 'Over there.'

'Can I come to your place?'

He knew it would be okay with his mum. 'Sure, but you'd better let Julie know.'

'I'll message her.' She didn't wait for an answer to her text. 'Come on,' she said, pushing off down the hill.

Hesse followed. It was a still evening but the air had cooled, and it cut straight through him. Fenna accelerated away, crouching low over the bars, her hips riding just above the seat. He pedalled hard to catch up as she disappeared around the corner near the Fat Controller.

She waited for him in front of the general store, then they climbed the hill towards home. Most of the houses in his street were holiday places, so his was one of the few with lights on.

Imogen was sitting at the kitchen table with a cup of chai. The cinnamon smell filled the room.

'Have you eaten?' This was the first question she asked any young person who walked through her door. She was good at welcoming people into their home. 'How was the surf?' she asked.

Hesse hadn't told her they were going surfing, but he guessed their wet hair was a giveaway. 'Pretty good—and no we haven't eaten,' he said. 'You remember Fenna?'

'Hello, honey. You look wet through.'

Fenna was shivering and her clothes were still damp.

'Go in by the fire,' Imogen said to Fenna. 'Warm up a bit.'

Hesse opened the concertina doors to the lounge room and the heat spilled over them. The weatherboard cottage slumped a little on its foundations. The floorboards creaked and it moaned like an old ship on windy nights. An entire wall of the lounge room was lined with bookshelves and the room smelled of incense and wood smoke.

Fenna took it all in. 'So nice,' she said.

'It's a bit rundown, but we like it,' Hesse said.

'Have you ever been inside the Turners' place?' she asked. 'It's like a…I'm not sure how you say it…a house from a magazine.'

'A display home,' he said.

'*Ja.*'

She stood in front of the fire and rubbed the backs of her legs through her tights. She was shaking her head.

'What?' he asked.

'The fire!'

'So?'

'No one has these at home. They're so bad for the environment.'

'It looks like you don't mind it now,' Hesse said.

She smiled. 'I love a fire,' she said. 'Doesn't everyone?'

Fenna's phone rang. She pulled it from her pocket, looked at the screen and sighed. Hesse guessed who it might be.

Imogen hustled him out, and they closed the doors to give her some privacy. Fenna kept her voice low but Hesse could still hear. 'I'm at Hesse's place…I know, but…it was cold, so…yes, his mum is here…okay, okay!' She hung up abruptly and pulled open the doors. 'I have to go,' she said.

'Okay,' Hesse said, struggling to hide his disappointment.

'I'll see you tomorrow, huh?' she said. 'On the bus?'

He'd almost forgotten she'd be at Castlereagh High. 'Sure,' he said.

'Be careful riding home,' Imogen said. 'Do you have a light on your bike?'

She hesitated. 'No, but I'll be okay,' she said.

'I could go with you,' Hesse offered.

'No, I'll be fine,' Fenna said.

'It's no bother,' Hesse insisted.

Imogen gave him a knowing look. 'Straight back home, okay?'

A mist had fallen and the streetlights created little haloes of orange as Fenna and Hesse rode down towards Ocean Road. They didn't speak until he drew up next to her where the road flattened out along the river.

'You didn't have to do this,' she said.

'It's a dangerous town, Shelbourne,' he replied. 'Murderers, kidnappers, stalkers, we've got them all. It's a hotbed of crime.'

'The only dangerous thing is the freaking cold!' she said.

Outside the pub a chalkboard advertised parmas and pots for ten bucks. The lights from the bar glowed warmly and the poker machines flashed in the gaming room. They swung away from the river and climbed the hill towards the Turners' place.

Hesse was fit but Fenna matched him all the way up. She dismounted at the gate and leaned towards him. 'Thank you for the surfing lesson. I've had my best day in Australia so far,' she said.

'And how long have you been here?' he asked.

She stopped and counted. 'Seven days.'

'Not much competition, then.'

The porch light came on and Julie Turner opened the front door. She didn't say anything, just stood watching.

Fenna nodded towards her. 'Aunt Lydia is waiting,' she said.

Hesse smiled. He'd watched *The Handmaid's Tale* with Imogen.

'See you tomorrow,' she said, reaching out and squeezing his arm. 'What time is the bus?'

'Seven forty-five outside the newsagents.'

She nodded, pushed open the gate and wheeled her bike to the shed.

Hesse stood for a moment, watching her. The weekend had been a blur because of her. It seemed impossible he'd only met her on Friday.

5

There was no shelter at the bus stop, just the bare footpath at the front of Spencer's newsagency. The Castlereagh High bus pulled up there, but the Hastings Girls College bus had its own stop, with a shelter, fifty metres down the road. Kids gathered in small groups according to uniform, the high schoolers in green and grey—the boys in shorts, the girls in long pants—and the college girls in maroon blazers and pleated skirts.

Hesse looked for Fenna as soon as he arrived, but she was nowhere to be seen. There were the usual Monday-morning conversations about footy and netball and surfing as the high school kids huddled together on the footpath. Mr Spencer didn't allow them to browse in the newsagency while they waited for the bus. They reciprocated by taking it in turns to activate the automatic doors every twenty seconds or so, letting the cold morning air into his shop.

Hesse stood with Mustafa and Jacob. They'd been in Shelbourne a couple of years, part of a government rural resettlement plan for refugees. The irony of them moving to the coast was that they were both afraid of the sea.

'If you want to be eaten by a shark,' Mus had told Hesse early on, 'that's up to you. But I like my arms and legs attached.'

Jake's dad was a truck driver at the mine and Mus's mum did the cleaning at the pub and half a dozen other businesses in town.

'What happened to you?' Jake asked, pointing to Hesse's face. The swelling had eased but his eye was darker.

'Just an accident,' Hesse replied. 'How'd you go on Saturday?' Jake was the number-one ruckman for the under-seventeens footy team, by virtue of being ten centimetres taller than any other kid his age.

'Beaten soundly. Again,' Jake said. His English was very polite. Anyone else would have said they were *flogged*. It had taken Jake six months to accept the shortening of his name. 'Why do you call me this?' he would ask. 'My name is Jacob?'

'Dunno,' Hesse had said. 'Everyone's name gets shortened.'

'Yours is not shortened,' Jake had replied.

'There's not much you can do with Hesse. There's nowhere to go with it.'

Mus wore two jumpers and a scarf pulled up to cover his mouth. But he wore shorts all year round. His legs were covered with thick, dark hair; he was the hairiest seventeen-year-old

Hesse had ever met. Castlereagh High had a policy of not allowing facial hair and the kids joked that Mus had to shave at recess and lunch just to conform.

'Did you finish your essay for Dalgety's class?' he asked Hesse.

'Nearly. What about you?'

Mus's spoken English was good, but he found writing hard. 'Same,' he said.

They watched as a big four-wheel drive with a *Hadron* sign on the door, pulled into a parking bay opposite the bus stop. Hesse knew the car. Felicity Holden's dad, Terry, was the manager at the mine. Felicity was the same age as Hesse and went to Hastings Girls. Her family had been in town for about five years but he had barely spoken to her in that time. He couldn't tell whether she was up herself or shy. Either way, she hadn't made many friends in Shelbourne.

As she stepped down from the front seat of the car, everyone stared. Felicity was tall, blonde and, Hesse had to admit, beautiful. But that's not what had caught their attention. She wasn't wearing her maroon blazer and skirt but a grey Castlereagh High uniform. She lifted her schoolbag onto her shoulder and slammed the door. She hesitated then walked towards Hesse and the others.

'What?' she said to no one in particular.

Further down the street, all the Hastings girls had turned to look.

Tina Best stepped forward. 'What the actual fuck?' she said. Tina had a way with words. She was captain of the girls' footy team and built like a fridge. She preferred to go through her opponents rather than around them. Most of the boys would have been afraid to play against her. Her dad was an electrician at the mine.

'Good morning to you too, Tina,' Felicity replied. Her dad backed out and tooted the horn but Felicity ignored him.

Tina straightened like she was bracing for heavy contact. 'Things going well at home then?'

Felicity stepped around her and swept through the newsagency door. Mr Spencer, who knew a genuine customer when he saw one, greeted her with a smile.

'What do you think has happened?' Jake asked.

Hesse had no idea. He was more interested in where Fenna was. She should have been here by now. The bus arrived, swinging through the car park and lurching to a halt in front of them.

'Still on your Ps?' Tina said to the driver as she bustled up the steps. Mr Brown had been driving the bus for as long as Hesse had been catching it. In that time there'd been half a dozen near misses, a stop sign knocked clean out of the ground and a parked car sideswiped. Browny's big, round frame barely fitted behind the steering wheel, which seemed to disappear into the folds of his stomach. He knew all the kids by name and he never pulled away from the stop without telling a dad joke.

Felicity was the last one to get on, a new magazine tucked under her arm. She had a quick, terse conversation with Browny about getting a bus pass from school then walked down the aisle, uncertain of her standing. Everybody had their designated seats, older kids at the back, younger ones at the front. Tina was sitting in a double seat on her own but moved to spread herself across both. Jake was the politest person Hesse knew. He pushed his large frame closer to the window and nodded to Felicity. She looked relieved and sat down with her bag on her lap. Hesse and Mus were sitting behind her. There was still no sign of Fenna.

Browny swung around in his seat with a broad smile. No one was really sure if he wore a hairpiece, but sometimes his hair seemed to move independently of his head. 'Did you hear I got mugged by six dwarves on the weekend?' he said. The kids waited for the punchline. 'Yeah,' he said. 'Not Happy.'

A collective groan filled the bus. Browny was oblivious. 'Not Happy,' he said again, louder this time.

'Yeah, we got it the first time,' Tina called from the back.

Mondays always started with an assembly in the gym and a speech from the principal, Mrs Shawshank, that was supposed to inspire students to be their best, followed by a rundown on the week ahead from the year-level coordinators. Shawshank wasn't one for underdressing. Everything she wore made a statement—huge earrings, red lipstick and brightly coloured clothes. Today's outfit was a big dress contained at the waist by a wide black belt.

'Nice dress,' Tina said. 'Looks like someone threw up on a three-man tent.'

The speech washed over virtually everybody, teachers included. The gym was cold at this time of year and Hesse, Jake and Mus fidgeted, trying to get comfortable on the hard parquetry floor. The only time Hesse paid any attention was when Fenna's name was mentioned.

'And we are very pleased to welcome our exchange student from the Netherlands.' Mrs Shawshank said. 'Fenna, can you come up to the front please.' Everyone craned their necks waiting for Fenna to show herself.

The principal waited. Conversations broke out around the gym.

'Thank you, students, that's enough. It seems Fenna isn't with us today, but I'm sure you will all make her welcome when you meet her.'

Hesse felt strangely happy he didn't have to share her with anyone yet. He thought about their surf lesson the day before—just the two of them, the beach, the surf, the way her damp clothes clung to her body on the ride home.

Period one was English with Mr Dalgety. Hesse hadn't quite finished his essay but thought he could scratch together a concluding paragraph while Dalgety talked. The school liked to place the Shelbourne kids in the same home room, so Felicity had joined his class. Hesse hoped that meant Fenna would too.

Mr Dalgety looked permanently tired in the way only a fifty-year-old teacher could. There was something crumpled about him, defeated. Hesse had the impression he would go home at night and mark off the days on his bedroom wall, like a prisoner in his cell, until his retirement. Tufts of greying hair clung to the sides of his balding head, and his clothes always looked a couple of sizes too big. For all that though, there were times when he was animated and enthusiastic, like when he read aloud from Hemingway or they did a film study of *Dead Poet's Society*. There was a scene at the end where the students all stood on their desks and said something about the teacher being their captain. Dalgety's eyes would glaze over, and he'd hold a hand to his heart like he was in love.

'And how did you all go with the essay on climate change?' he began. 'I'd like to hear about some of the issues you researched.' He often started his classes like this, no introductions, just straight into it like fifty minutes wouldn't be enough time to get through everything he had planned.

The class fell silent. Hesse guessed a lot of them would be asking for an extension.

Mus put his hand up. 'I think the planet is in deep trouble,' he said.

'How so, Mustafa?' Mr Dalgety had taken up his customary position, sitting on the front of his desk, his legs on a chair.

'Well, if we want to limit warming to below two degrees, we should be acting now. But we're not doing nearly enough.'

Dalgety crossed his arms. 'The government has policies in place. There's an emissions reduction target. What more would you like to see?'

Mus shrugged.

'We need to stop burning fossil fuels,' Hesse said. He thought back to the meeting on Friday night. 'We have to switch to renewables much faster than we are—wind, solar. It's not like they're in short supply in Australia.'

Felicity's hand shot into the air.

Dalgety checked the roll for her name. 'Yes, Felicity.'

'The jury is still out on climate change,' Felicity began, directing her comments at Hesse. 'The earth has gone through cycles of warming before and this could just be another one. We did a whole unit on it at Hastings last term. We had actual scientists come and speak to us.'

'Ooh,' Tina said. '*Actual* scientists.'

Hesse couldn't help himself. 'The science is proven, or as much as it can be,' he said. 'If ninety-five per cent of climate scientists tell me the planet is warming, I reckon that's good enough for me.'

Felicity wasn't impressed. 'Climate scientists!' she said. 'My dad says they just want the research money.'

'You mean NASA?' Hesse asked. 'Or the UN? They're all just after the money?'

'My dad's an engineer,' Felicity replied. 'He knows what he's talking about.'

Hesse was getting fired up now. 'Can I ask you something?'

'Of course,' she said, confidently.

Hesse scrambled to remember an analogy he'd read on the weekend about the science. 'If you had a toothache and nine dentists all said you needed a filling, but a plumber told you it looked okay, would you believe the plumber?'

The class laughed.

Felicity smirked. 'Of course not. I'd have the filling.'

'But you'd believe an engineer, before you'd believe NASA.'

'It's a stupid analogy,' Felicity said.

'No, it's the same. You just have to believe the science,' Hesse said.

'Climate change is a theory. It hasn't been fully proven.'

Mus found his voice. 'What about gravity, do you believe in that? It's just a theory isn't it, Mr Dalgety?'

'It's a very well developed theory.' Dalgety seemed happy to let the debate continue.

'And, anyway,' Hesse said to Felicity, 'your dad manages a coalmine. He's no expert on climate change.'

'Oh, so now you personalise the argument. Well done. It's my dad's fault,' she said.

'Felicity is right, Hesse,' Mr Dalgety said. 'There's no need to get personal.'

'But her dad's biased.'

'The mine provides jobs,' Felicity said. 'It employs a lot of people in Shelbourne.' She may have been new to the school—and to this class—but she wasn't afraid to speak up. 'How many of your parents work for Hadron?' she asked, looking around the room.

Half a dozen kids put their hands up, including Jake and Tina, reluctantly.

'And what about all the other businesses in town that rely on the mine for their income?' Felicity continued. 'Not to mention the clubs it pours money into. Hadron keeps Shelbourne afloat. It'd die without it.'

There was something about the way she said this, the finality of it, like no one else could have a different opinion, that got under Hesse's skin.

'You've lived in Shelbourne for five minutes,' he said. 'There's so much more to it than just a dirty coalmine and power station.'

'That produces power you use!' Felicity cut in.

Hesse ignored her. 'We've got the bush and the ocean and great surf.'

'And how many jobs do they provide?' Felicity said.

'Tourism provides jobs,' Hesse replied. 'But why does it always have to be about jobs?'

'Because people need to eat,' she said. 'And to eat they need money, and to get money they need work. It's pretty simple. I would have thought even you could understand that.'

There was a collective intake of breath. The rest of the class was enjoying the argument, swinging between Hesse and Felicity as they traded blows.

'So,' Hesse said, 'it's okay to continue to dig up the earth, to destroy the environment and pollute the air, as long as there are jobs in it?'

'It's called progress,' Felicity said. 'And it keeps the economy growing.'

'And what happens to the economy when there's nothing left to dig up, no clean water to drink, no air we can breathe?'

A knowing smile slid across Felicity's lips. She sighed. 'Alarmists. That's what my dad calls people like you. The sky is falling! The sky is falling!' She looked around for someone to laugh along with her, but she'd misread the room. She was too new, too sure of herself for anyone to side with her yet.

'Okay, okay,' Dalgety said. 'That's enough. I'm impressed with the research you've all done. I hope it's reflected in your essays.'

Half the class couldn't meet his gaze.

~

The ride home on the bus was always quieter—earbuds in, eyes locked on screens. Felicity sat up the front and was the first off when they arrived in Shelbourne.

The wind had turned onshore, so Hesse was in no hurry. There wouldn't be any surf today. Imogen was working a late shift, meaning he'd be cooking again. He said goodbye to Jake and Mus and walked towards the supermarket. He'd just about run out of ideas for pasta sauces. It would be so much easier if his mum wasn't vegetarian—he could buy some chops and spuds and dinner would be covered. He wandered the aisles looking for inspiration but knew he'd end up making lentil slop again—Imogen's favourite comfort food, a big pot of slow-cooked lentils and veggies. At least it was cheap and easy to prepare.

As he turned into the vegetable section, he saw Fenna. She was standing in front of the fruit display holding a bag of oranges.

'Hey,' he said, walking up to her.

She looked at him as though she didn't recognise him. Her eyes were glazed and her shoulders slumped.

'*Hai*,' she said finally. Her voice was slow, totally different to the sparky girl from yesterday.

'Are you okay?' he asked, touching her arm.

She pulled away. 'I've got to go,' she said and walked quickly towards the checkout.

Hesse followed her. 'Are you sure you're all right?'

She turned on him. 'I am *fine*. Please leave me alone.'

She dropped the bag of oranges next to the newspapers and ran out the door. Other shoppers stopped and stared. Hesse considered following her but she clearly didn't want to speak to him. He went back to the vegetable section, wondering what he'd done wrong.

He didn't see Jago until he was at the checkout. He wore grease-stained coveralls and carried three steaks in plastic trays, two loaves of white bread and a bottle of milk.

Hesse emptied his basket onto the counter: carrots, potatoes, capsicum, onion, garlic and a can of tomatoes.

'That eye's still not looking good,' Jago said. 'You should be more careful.'

Hesse ignored him. The checkout girl hadn't smiled at Hesse in three years and she wasn't about to start today. She looked blankly at him, weighed each item and slid it along the counter. 'Do you want a bag?' she asked, her voice flat.

'No, I'm right, thanks.' He shoved his purchases into his school backpack, paid and turned for the door.

'You have a good one,' she said, in the same monotone.

'Saw your Dutchie friend just now,' Jago called after him. 'Had a chat. Told her I'd show her around.'

Hesse had had enough disappointments for one day—Fenna hadn't been at school and now she'd just brushed him off, he'd lost the argument with Felicity in English and Jago was on his case again. They weighed on him as he trudged up the Russell Street hill.

The house was cold. He'd have to split some wood and get the fire going later, but for now, he just wanted to blow off some energy. He pulled his mountain bike out of the shed and checked the tyres.

'Hesse.' Fenna's voice was low and soft but it made him jump.

'Shit,' he said. 'You scared the bejesus out of me.'

She was sitting on the bench at the side of the shed. She pushed her hoodie back and her hair spilled across her face. Her eyes were smudged and dark.

'What's up?' Hesse asked.

She shook her head. 'I'm sorry for snapping at you. I don't know what's happening to me.'

Hesse eased down next to her. 'What do you mean?'

'I'm all screwed up. It wasn't supposed to be like this.'

'Like what?'

'Forget it. It's not your problem.' She got up and walked slowly across the yard.

'Wait,' Hesse said.

She stopped and turned, picking at the stitching on her sleeve. Then she sat down, cross-legged on the grass and cupped her face in her palms.

Hesse cautiously moved towards her and dropped to his knees. 'You don't have to talk,' he said.

'I'm all over the place,' she said. She spoke so softly Hesse couldn't tell if she was talking to herself or to him. 'I don't mean to hurt people, but I do. I've been really good the past six months. I thought I'd worked it out.'

'Worked what out?'

She looked up at him briefly, her gaze assessing. '*Angst*, you know this word?'

'Like, anxiety, you mean.'

'*Ja*. Anxiety.'

Hesse struggled to think of anything to say. He liked Fenna but he didn't want to push her. He felt for her though—arriving in a new country, being dumped with the Turners—he guessed that must be hard.

'Maybe you just need to give it some time?' he ventured.

'I wish it was that easy. Everything is new here and everyone expects me to be smart and clever and to speak well. But, right now, I just can't. All I want is to sit in my room and not talk to anyone.' She looked up at him, assessing again. 'You wouldn't understand.'

'Try me,' he persisted.

'You'll laugh at me,' she said.

'I won't, I promise.'

The words spilled out of her then, like they'd been dammed up waiting for a moment of release. 'It's feeling like you're being watched and judged all the time—and knowing you're never good enough. It's worrying the whole time that bad things will happen. It's always sitting at the back of the room. It's desperately wanting to go to a party but not being able to walk in the door. It's not dressing pretty because it'll draw attention. It's always leaving without saying goodbye. And running away. Lots of running away.'

'But yesterday at the beach?'

'I know. Sometimes I'm okay,' she said. 'And yesterday was a good day. I just don't know when the bad days are coming. I can't predict them.'

'And being somewhere new doesn't help.'

'*Ja*,' she said, finally lifting her head to look at him. 'Just now, in the supermarket, that boy from the hotel—'

'Jago?'

'He was so close, looking at me and questioning me. I didn't like him doing that. Not on a bad day. I shouldn't have but I pushed him back.'

'You shoved Jago!' Hesse almost laughed. 'I wish I'd seen that.'

'I feel like I'm struggling to find…' She waved her hand in the air, searching for the words.

'Where you fit in?'

'*Ja*, where I fit in. And it's so hard to speak English all the time.'

'Your English is better than my Dutch,' he said.

'You speak Dutch?'

'Sure.'

'I don't believe you,' she said. Some of the tension seemed to have left her body. She almost smiled.

'Gouda,' he said, trying not to laugh.

'That's it? That's all you've got? Cheese?'

'It's a start, isn't it?'

She reached over and punched his arm. 'You are the nicest *idioot* I have met,' she said.

'So,' he said, 'is that why you weren't at school today? You were nervous.'

'Nervous?' She shook her head. '*Nee*, it's much worse than that. Sometimes it takes over my whole body, you know? My heart races. I can't breathe, like someone is standing on my chest. I just have to get away. Wherever I am.'

'Like a panic attack?'

'*Ja*, they are the worst.'

Hesse thought she was relaxing the longer they talked. 'So, how do you manage it back at home?'

'Yoga. Swimming. Lots of things.'

Hesse remembered helping her into the wetsuit, her swimmer's shoulders.

'Have you been talking to your parents?'

She took out her phone and tapped the screen, bringing up messages to her parents. She scrolled through about thirty texts, all in Dutch. 'And that's just today,' she said.

'Can I do anything to help?' he asked.

She sighed. 'You are so nice, but it's not like being a friend can fix it. I just need to balance things better.'

'And you're worried about going to school.' Hesse thought of the assembly that morning, how Mrs Shawshank had called her out.

She nodded. 'Everyone will be looking at me, asking me questions. They will want me to speak in front of people.'

'You must have expected that.'

'*Ja*, of course. And I'll be okay. I just need to see a doctor for a script.'

Hesse's heart gave a little jolt. She was on meds. 'But you don't know who to see?' he asked. He thought of Ruby, the young doctor at the meeting the other night. 'I think I know someone.'

63

'Thanks, but the doctor isn't the problem. It's getting the script filled at the *apotheek*.'

Hesse had forgotten Colin Turner was the local chemist. 'I get it, but surely you have to tell him anyway. He's your host.'

She shook her head. 'It's not supposed to be permanent, remember. If they find me a new family, maybe I'll tell them.'

It was growing colder. The onshore had pushed low, scudding clouds in off the strait. Fenna pulled the hoodie back over her head and tucked her hands into the sleeves. 'Can I come in for a while?' she asked.

'Sure,' Hesse said. 'Why don't you stay for dinner? Mum'll be home later, she's on afternoon shift.'

'Thank you.'

Hesse was on his feet. 'I'll get the fire going before we freeze our tits off.'

She looked up at him. 'You say the strangest things.'

'Just an expression,' he said, a little embarrassed.

'It's okay. I like it. *Freeze our tits off.*' She exaggerated his accent again and made him laugh.

6

Fenna squatted next to Hesse while he set the fire. Once he had it going she stretched her hands towards the flames.

'Can I help with dinner?' she asked.

Hesse thought she seemed a little more relaxed. Neither of them spoke as they peeled and chopped the veggies. A couple of times they bumped elbows and she smiled. As the kitchen warmed, she took off her hoodie. She wore a black T-shirt with KENSINGTON written across the front.

'Kensington?' he asked.

'Oh, you have to hear them. They are so great.' She pulled the phone from her pocket, scrolled for a few seconds and turned the volume up.

She started swaying to the music. 'What do you think?'

She could have put anything on, and he would have answered the same way. 'I like it,' he said. He was under the spell of this girl dancing in his kitchen, her arms above her head, her hair flying around her face.

'Come on,' she said, reaching her hands out to him.

Hesse had always been a reluctant dancer. It was bad enough being a gangly seventeen-year-old, all elbows and knees, but dancing magnified his clumsiness. Imogen called his awkward attempts the footy-club shuffle—employed once a year at the school social. Still, here was Fenna, all curves and smooth skin, beckoning him towards her. She took his hand. Every part of her seemed to move in sync, her shoulders lifting, her arms sliding back and away, her hips swaying. He just wanted to watch her.

The song faded but still she danced.

'So,' she said, smiling. 'There're two things I have to teach you: how to ice skate and how to dance.'

He had already stopped and crossed his arms.

She sighed. 'I love dancing. The music changes the way I feel about myself. It's like swimming.'

They returned to chopping the veggies. Hesse sautéed the onions and garlic and the kitchen filled with the smell of the spices he added, while the lentils boiled in a separate pot.

'It's getting dark,' Hesse said. 'You should ring Julie, let her know where you are.'

'I'll text her,' Fenna said.

'No, call her.'

'Why?'

'Things are not great with you two, are they?'

'How did you guess?' she said sarcastically.

'So, make like you're being the considerate one. Adults love that shit. Tell her you're doing some homework with me.'

'Homework when I haven't been to school yet?'

'I hadn't thought of that. Maybe say it's some sort of induction thing the school asked me to do with you. Because we both live in Shelbourne.'

Fenna stepped outside to make the call. Hesse tried to listen, but she kept her voice low. When she came back in, she seemed pleased with herself. 'It worked!'

She looked around the kitchen as though she was seeing it for the first time. 'I like it here so much,' she said. 'And your mum is so nice.'

'Yeah, I guess she is.'

'Where is your dad?'

Hesse had told the story so many times over the years he'd learned to contain it to a single sentence. 'He died when I was ten—drowned surfing.'

Her eyes widened.

It was one of the ways he judged people—how they responded when he told them about his dad. Some missed the message he sent with the shortness of his explanation. They wanted details—the when, how and why—as though it was a story on the evening news.

Now, it felt like Fenna looked right into him, knowing intuitively it was something he preferred not to talk about.

'I'm so sorry,' she said.

'It's okay. It was a long time ago.'

She nodded, but still her eyes held him.

Hesse turned away from her gaze and checked the dinner. He drained the lentils in the sink and added them to the pot of veggies, along with a can of tomatoes. 'And there you have it,' he said. 'Lentil slop.'

They sat on the floor by the fire and waited for Imogen to come home before eating. Hesse was still trying to figure Fenna out. She seemed to change in front of his eyes. Only a couple of hours ago she virtually ignored him in the supermarket, and yet here she was, animated and leading the conversation with no sign of the anxiety she'd talked about.

'Hello, you two,' Imogen said, bustling through the back door and unwrapping herself from the scarf and coat she wore over her uniform. She didn't seem surprised to find Fenna there. She lifted the lid on the pot and checked the stew, inhaling the warm, spicy aroma. 'Thanks for getting dinner organised,' she said.

'I had some help,' Hesse said.

If his mum had asked him what they'd been talking about for the last hour, he'd have struggled to remember anything specific. They both got to their feet and Imogen gave Hesse a peck on the cheek. Turning to Fenna, she opened her arms as though they were old friends. 'And it's so lovely to see you again,' she said, giving her a hug.

Fenna glanced at Hesse over his mum's shoulder. Her eyes were glistening.

'How was your first day at school?' Imogen asked Fenna.

Hesse jumped in. 'Come on, Mum, we're starving. We've been waiting for you.'

The moment slipped and Hesse got Fenna to help him serve. He sliced some of Imogen's homemade bread, ladled the soup into three bowls and handed two to Fenna. 'So, what's happening with the campaign, Mum?' Hesse asked.

Imogen left a long enough pause for him to realise she knew he was directing the conversation away from school. 'I'm sure Fenna doesn't want to talk about that,' she said.

'*Ja*, I do,' Fenna said. 'Hesse has been telling me about it.'

'Has he?' Imogen said, smiling pointedly at him.

Hesse slurped his soup.

'I spoke to Oliver today. You remember him, the lawyer?' Imogen began.

'Yeah. He talks a lot,' Hesse said.

'He thinks we need to call a bigger meeting. Get the wider community involved. He's contacted a couple of environment groups in Melbourne and they want to help.'

'Is that what we want? Wouldn't it be better if we kept it local?' Hesse asked.

'Did you say *we*? So, you're on board now?'

Hesse shrugged. 'It's a bit hard to avoid when all the meetings are held here.'

Fenna nodded. 'It seems like…'

'What?' Imogen said, encouraging her.

'It's like stepping back in time here. You still have open fires, you have a coalmine on your back doorstep. And you have arguments about whether climate change is real or not.' Hesse had told her about the debate in Mr Dalgety's class.

'You're right.' Imogen didn't sound offended. 'But we're waking up. Slowly.'

'I'm sorry,' Fenna said. 'I didn't mean to be rude.'

'No, it's okay,' Imogen said. 'I guess it's because we're a small country, population-wise.'

'But Australia is the highest emitter per capita in the world.'

'You've been doing your homework!' Hesse was looking at Fenna in a new light.

'Of course. I had to sit an exam before I could come here,' she said. 'We studied Australian politics, environment, culture, customs.'

'But not the weather?' Hesse said.

'I must have fallen asleep in that class.'

'Sounds like you're both joining the campaign,' Imogen said.

'It's not going to be easy, Mum.' Hesse told her about the argument with Felicity.

'Hang on, Felicity Holden is at Castlereagh High!' Imogen said. 'How did that happen?'

'Dunno. She just turned up at the bus stop this morning. No explanation.'

'Maybe Terry Holden's job is under threat, if his daughter has moved to the high school,' Imogen said.

'Who knows?' Hesse continued. 'Anyway, lots of kids in town have parents working at Hadron. Jake's dad included. It took him ages to find that job.'

'I know,' Imogen said. 'But we've put up with Hadron for

too long. If they can't find a buyer, they could be forced to shut down at last.'

'And put eighty people out of work.'

'Most of the workers aren't from Shelbourne, they come from all over.'

'Does that matter?' Hesse said, a little annoyed that he was sounding like Felicity.

'I guess not,' Imogen said. 'But like Fenna says, we can't pretend to be concerned about climate change and have a dirty coalmine in our backyard.'

'But the shit will hit the fan, Mum,' Hesse replied. 'It's not just the jobs. There are all the clubs in town that get money from Hadron. They won't want to give that up.'

'They've been sucking on the teat of Hadron for years,' Imogen said, smiling at the image. She saw Fenna was struggling to keep up with the conversation. 'Sorry.'

'It's okay,' Fenna said. 'You talk so fast. And I don't understand "the shit will hit the fan".'

'It's pretty gross when you think about it,' Hesse said. 'I meant there'll be a backlash if the campaign goes ahead.'

'Oh, we're going ahead, all right,' Imogen said firmly. 'Oliver wants to hold the meeting on the long weekend.'

'That's only two weeks away,' Hesse said.

'The power station has been on the market for a month already. We need to get active before they find a buyer. Besides, I think you're overreacting. Things won't get too hostile in town. Everyone knows everyone. It's not like we're going to turn on each other.'

'I wouldn't be so sure about that.' Hesse told her about his run in with Stanton up at the mine fence.

'He took your photo?' Imogen said angrily. 'Why?'

'It all happened so quickly,' Hesse said. 'Anyway, what are the plans for this meeting?'

'We'll hold it on the Sunday afternoon. We're organising a speaker from Melbourne and a couple of locals will talk. Probably Oliver and Ruby.'

'That's dangerous,' Hesse said, 'giving Oliver a microphone.'

Imogen laughed. 'Yeah, I know what you mean,' she said. 'But he's a real asset to the campaign.'

After they'd helped Imogen clean up, Fenna put on her hoodie.

'Thank you for dinner,' she said.

Imogen held her by the shoulders. 'You're welcome,' she said. 'Anytime.'

Fenna kissed her three times on her cheeks, Dutch style.

This time there was no discussion about Hesse walking home with Fenna.

As they stepped out onto the back deck, Imogen touched Hesse on the sleeve. 'Straight back home, okay,' she said.

He nodded.

They walked in silence. A sliver of moon had risen and the Milky Way fanned out from horizon to horizon. Every few steps, Fenna would sway away from him then nudge back closer. Hesse watched as the streetlamps lit her face.

They crossed the bridge and followed the river trail, passing in and out of the shadows. He felt her hand, soft and cool, slide into his, entwining fingers. He almost leapt in the air with the exhilaration of it.

Still not having spoken a word, they turned up the hill towards the Turners' place. Halfway up she pulled him behind a parked car. She held his face and gently ran her thumb over his swollen eye. She pressed her lips against his.

'*Slaap lekker,*' she whispered.

She saw the look on his face.

'It means, sleep well,' she said.

Hesse doubted he would sleep at all, remembering the feeling of her lips on his.

Her hand slid from his face and she continued up the hill.

'See you at the bus tomorrow?' he called after her.

Fenna turned to face him, walking backwards. She gave him a little wave.

'Maybe,' she said.

7

Hesse didn't see Fenna for the rest of the week. He waited for her at the bus stop each morning, reluctantly taking his seat when she didn't turn up. Rumours swirled around school about the exchange girl: she'd changed her mind and gone home, she was pregnant and only came to Australia to get away, she couldn't speak a word of English.

Hesse didn't bother correcting them. He told Jake and Mus about the surf lesson he'd given Fenna, but not much more. Neither of them was curious. He guessed they knew what it was like to arrive somewhere completely new.

'She'll come when she's ready,' Mus said.

Hesse kept an eye out for her around Shelbourne—at the supermarket, on the beach—but she seemed to have disappeared as quickly as she'd arrived. He kicked himself for not having asked for her number. He walked to the Turners' place after school on Thursday, but no one answered when he knocked. There was no movement of the curtains in the front room, no sound of voices in the house. He even went into the chemist shop to see Mr Turner, but he was busy with customers.

In the meantime, Hesse's place had become the focal point for the campaign. Imogen switched her shifts to be home in the evening when the meetings were held. Oliver Bairstow turned out to be a high-flying Melbourne lawyer. Even when he was talking in their kitchen, he sounded like he was addressing a jury. He understood the climate science and he was smarter than just about anybody in the room, with the possible exception of Ruby. Hesse was blown away by the information he seemed to have at his fingertips—statistics about sea-level rise, carbon dioxide parts per million, emissions from the power station and the air monitoring done by Hadron.

Before the meeting on Friday night Hesse helped Imogen clean the place up a bit. He honestly couldn't tell the difference between a vacuumed rug and an unvacuumed one, but he knew his mum could.

'Any word from Fenna?' Imogen asked as he scrunched sheets of newspaper to set the fire.

'Nope. Nothing.'

'Is there something you're not telling me?' Imogen asked. She stood above him, one hand leaning on the mantelpiece.

'What makes you say that?' he asked, busying himself with the kindling to avoid looking at her.

'I dunno, maybe the inordinate care you're taking to light the fire there. You've rearranged the kindling five times so far.'

Hesse sometimes wondered if being a single parent with an only child gave her extra powers. Maybe concentrating all her energy on him allowed her to see things regular parents couldn't.

'She's just struggling with some stuff, Mum, that's all.'

'Private stuff?'

'Yeah. The sort of thing she wouldn't want to get out.'

'Well, you tread cautiously then, young man.' This is what she called him when she was being extra serious. 'She's obviously vulnerable and we wouldn't want anyone taking advantage of that, would we?'

'No,' he said. 'We wouldn't.'

It was a smaller meeting. Along with Oliver, Ruby and Bear, there were half a dozen people Hesse recognised from around town: Bob Young from the surf school, Eliza Wadsworth, whose daughter went to Hastings Girls and four others who looked familiar, but Hesse didn't know by name.

They'd decided to call the community meeting a forum.

'The wording is important,' Oliver said. 'We want it to be a place where everyone feels they can be heard.'

'And what if workers from Hadron turn up?' Eliza asked. 'Do we let them speak?'

'We have to be ready to counter their arguments no matter

where they post them. They've been getting a free run in the local paper.'

Since the announcement of the sale, there had been three articles in *The Chronicle* talking up the benefits of the mine and power station for Shelbourne, the jobs and the flow-on to local businesses. Hadron was waging its own campaign.

'How do we counter that sort of influence?' Bear asked.

'This argument isn't going to be won or lost in Shelbourne,' Oliver said. 'A buyer could come from anywhere around the world. Most big energy companies are multinational. That's where the ultimate decisions will be made.'

'So why bother with a local campaign?' Hesse asked. He had found himself being drawn into the meetings. What he really wanted was some ammunition to take Felicity down. She'd owned him in the argument in English and he didn't like it.

'Social licence,' Oliver said. 'It's what enables a company to operate with the acceptance of the community. A local campaign can undermine the social licence if the town starts to question whether it really wants Hadron—or any other company—here.'

'Hadron knows exactly how to make itself indispensable to a small town like Shelbourne,' Ruby continued. 'When golfers or lawn bowlers or netballers see Hadron signs plastered all over their new clubhouse, their fences and equipment, they don't think about the air their kids are breathing, or the connection with climate change—they just think how awesome the company is for supporting them.'

Hesse wasn't sure any of his mates cared where the money

came from, as long as they had good grounds and courts to play on and hot showers after the game.

'It's great that you are taking an interest, by the way,' Ruby said to Hesse.

'We've been studying climate change at school,' he replied.

Ruby smiled. She turned to Oliver. 'What do you think about—?'

'Yes!' Oliver said. 'Having a young person speak at the forum could be really powerful.'

'Woah, wait a minute.' Hesse realised they were talking about him. 'No way! I'm no public speaker. I'd be useless in front of an audience like that.'

'You were on the debating team at school,' Imogen said.

'Yeah, in year seven, Mum. That was ages ago. And I was rubbish at it.'

'I could help you prepare,' Oliver said.

'Put words in my mouth, you mean,' Hesse said.

'No,' Ruby said. 'Whatever you say would be your own words. It needs to be authentic. Will you at least think about it?'

Hesse was caught between being railroaded by Oliver and coaxed by Ruby. He wouldn't admit it, but he wanted to impress Ruby. He liked her calmness, the way she listened carefully before saying anything. 'It's not just the speaking,' he said. 'I've got mates whose parents work at Hadron.'

'It's a risk, nailing your colours to the mast in a small town,' Ruby replied. 'I could lose patients if they decide they don't like my stance.'

'We're all in the same boat,' Bob Young added.

'Maybe you should take some time to think about it,' Bear said. 'It's a big ask, standing up in front of an audience.'

'Bear's right,' Ruby said. 'But kids your age are getting much more active, Hesse.'

Hesse had heard about the School Strike for Climate rallies. There was a student environment group at Castlereagh High that lobbied the school council about stuff like recycling. They'd tried to advertise the next strike, but Mrs Shawshank had stopped them putting up posters.

'Okay, I'll think about it,' he said reluctantly.

'It's your decision, Hesse,' Ruby said.

He wished he'd spent the evening in his bedroom watching Netflix. A week ago, he hadn't given a second thought to Hadron, and now he was being pressured into speaking at a public meeting about shutting it down. Oliver could call it a forum if he liked but it could just as easily be a shitstorm—with Hesse right in the middle of it.

After the others had left, Bear stuck around. Imogen didn't seem to mind. Hesse had barely settled at his desk when she stuck her head through the door.

'Here,' she said, holding out a slip of paper.

'What's that?' he asked.

'Fenna's number,' she said.

'How? When?' he asked, standing to take it from her.

'I'm still capable of the odd surprise, you know.' She closed the door and headed back to the kitchen.

It was Friday night, ten-thirty.

He texted: *Hope you're doing okay. Hesse*

He lay back on the bed, his phone on the desk beside him. On still nights he liked to listen to the house groan as the old timbers stretched and settled. Tonight, the moaning of the wind through the sheoaks in the backyard meant the north-westerly was up and it'd be offshore in the morning. And, as always, there was the dull thrum of the power station turbines rolling down the valley.

He must have dozed off. The house was quiet when he woke to the buzzing of his phone.

'Hello.' His voice was dry and cracked with sleep.

No response.

'Fenna?'

'*Ja*,' she said. Barely a whisper.

'What time is it?' He pinched himself for saying something so dumb. What did it matter what time it was?

'I don't know. Late.'

'Where have you been all week?'

There was a long silence. 'This is all a mistake. I never should have come. I've been talking to my parents about going home.'

'Home? To the Netherlands?'

He thought he heard a little snort. '*Ja*. The Netherlands.'

'But—'

'I know. I've heard it all from Julie. I haven't even been to school yet.'

'Never thought I'd find myself agreeing with Aunt Lydia.'

Another snort. 'What should I do, Hesse?'

He hesitated. She was asking *him* what she should do. His mind scrambled for the right thing to say but all he could think about was the touch of her lips against his, her cool hands on his face. 'What did your parents say?'

'What you'd expect. Give it a chance, but if it's really bad, come home.'

'And is it really bad?'

'Not all of it. Not you.'

He wanted to hold that moment for as long as he could, but he was afraid she'd hang up. 'You've hardly met anyone yet. I'll introduce you to Jake and Mus. You'll like them.'

Silence again at her end.

He tried a new tack. 'Did you see the doctor?'

'*Ja*. She's nice. I told her you'd recommended her.'

Hesse thought of the way he'd caught Ruby looking at him a couple of times at the meeting tonight.

'And I found a chemist in Castlereagh yesterday,' Fenna continued. 'I went shopping with Julie. Told her I wanted to look around on my own for a while. She took me to the pool too. It was so good to swim again.'

'So, you're getting things sorted.'

There was a rustling noise on the line. A muffled voice. 'Sorry. I must have been talking in my sleep.'

Hesse waited, suddenly conscious of how fast his heart was beating.

'I have to go,' she whispered. 'Are you working tomorrow?'

Somehow, his heart found another gear. 'Yeah.'

'Okay.'

The line went dead.

Okay? What did that mean? Would she come to see him at

work? Should he text and ask what time?

Eventually, he switched his phone to silent, placed it face-down on the desk and replayed the conversation in his head. *Not you*, she'd said. Some things may be bad for her here, but not him.

8

Imogen was already up when Hesse walked into the kitchen in the morning. Her face had a glow Hesse couldn't ignore.

'You look happy,' he said.

'It's the weekend,' she replied, dropping two pieces of bread into the toaster.

'What time did Bear leave?' he asked without looking at her.

'What time did you finish talking to Fenna?' she replied, taking a jar of honey from the pantry cupboard.

'He's stayed late after a couple of meetings now.' He sliced a banana into his bowl of Weet-Bix.

She sat opposite him at the table. 'He's nice,' she said. 'We're friends. That's all.'

He lifted his palms to her. 'I wasn't saying anything. Just…'

'Just…?'

Suppressing a smile, he did his best to imitate her concerned-mother voice, 'Be careful with that guy.'

She laughed. 'Very funny, Hesse. Very funny.'

Hesse shovelled the cereal into his mouth like it was his last meal and someone was waiting for the bowl. 'Seriously, Mum,' he said between spoonfuls. 'It'd be good if you met someone.'

Hesse knew that every moment she had lived and worked and cooked and cleaned since his dad died had been for him. To see him happy and washed and fed and wearing half-decent clothes. And she'd told him more than once she hated that Hesse surfed. They had argued about it when he was younger but now she seemed resigned to it. Still, he was sure she said a silent prayer every time he loaded his board into his bike rack and headed for the beach. She tried to hide it but she was always relieved when he came home, his hair still wet, his face flushed from the ride and the energy drained from him by the surf. She loved the ocean, but it had taken her husband, stolen him away without even the chance of a goodbye. At ten years of age, Hesse had been too young to deal with anyone else's grief. It had only been in the last few years he'd come to understand his mum's loss was as deep as—if not deeper than—his own.

Imogen smiled and shook her head. 'Are you giving me advice now?'

'Not advice.' Milk dribbled down his chin and he wiped it with the back of his hand. 'Just, you know, it would be okay with me if you had a boyfriend.'

'I'm thirty-nine, Hesse. You don't have boyfriends at thirty-nine.'

'Okay, a relationship then. I wouldn't mind if you were in a relationship.'

She spread honey on her toast and sliced it in half. 'Yeah, maybe,' she said.

Theo was standing in the front door of the shop, waiting to set off to the Fat Controller.

Hesse parked his bike by the side of the shaping bay.

'Coffee?' Theo called.

'Yeah. A triple espresso, thanks. Hold the sugar.'

Theo stood at the corner with his hands on his hips. He was dressed in his usual attire: boardshorts, thongs and a hoodie, under which there may or may not have been a T-shirt. 'Really?' he asked.

'What do you reckon?' Hesse replied.

'Won't stop me asking? Now—'

'I know, roll the boards out and give the front a sweep. You've set up the till,' Hesse said.

Theo smiled and turned his back, heading for the cafe.

The morning was cloudy, and the surface of the river seemed to shiver in the breeze. The windsock on the roof rippled as if in expectation of the change due in the afternoon.

By the time Theo returned, Hesse had set up all the second-hand boards and swept the concrete skirt out to the footpath. It was still early but he couldn't help looking along the road towards the bridge—the direction Fenna would come from if she intended to stop in and see him. But the town was quiet, with just a trickle of cars passing the front door and the hum of a lawnmower in one of the side streets.

Theo perched himself behind the counter and savoured his coffee.

'You should buy yourself a coffee machine,' Hesse said. 'You'd save a fortune.'

'Yeah, I know. But there's something meditative about my morning walk down to the Fat Controller. I like the chat I have with Rachel while she makes my coffee. I'd miss that. It'd just be me, in a small room, making shit coffee.'

Hesse sorted through the wetsuit rack, looking for one from last season's stock that might fit Fenna a little better than his mum's.

'How's your week been?' Theo asked.

The swelling around Hesse's eye had all but disappeared and he was thankful it was no longer the first topic of conversation. He continued to flick through the wetsuits absent-mindedly while he filled Theo in on the developments in the campaign, including the plans for the forum on the long weekend.

'A forum?' Theo replied. 'Could be interesting if a few Hadron workers turn up.'

'Not only that,' Hesse said. 'They want me to speak.'

Whenever Theo raised his eyebrows, the rest of his face furrowed and the crow's feet around his eyes connected with the deep lines on his forehead. 'So, are you going to do it?' he asked.

'I don't really want to,' Hesse said, 'but it makes sense to have a young person speak. I just wish there was someone else they could ask.'

Theo thought on this for a while. 'Maybe you should give it a crack,' he said. 'What could go wrong?'

'Apart from making a complete idiot of myself, you mean?'

Theo smiled. 'A young bloke having a go—I reckon the crowd would be pretty forgiving.'

'Yeah, unless it turns into a total shitfest.'

Hesse spent most of the morning outside in the stripping bay next to the car park. When second-hand boards were dropped off for sale on consignment, he cleaned them up by scraping the wax off and fixing the dings. A little bit of love could increase the price by fifty dollars—and therefore the commission Theo charged for the sale.

He was working on a mini-mal that had seen better days when Jago's black ute swung into the car park and came to a halt in the gravel at the side of the shop. Seeing Hesse, Jago edged forward, the motor rumbling under the bonnet, his face hidden behind the tinted windscreen. Finally, he killed the motor and swung open the driver's door. Hesse could see the outline of someone in the passenger seat.

'Hey, Hesse, my man,' Jago called, sauntering towards him. 'There're no end to your talents, are there? It's good you've stayed at school long enough to learn how to scrape wax off a board.' It was the first time Jago had called him anything other than dipshit.

Jago stood with his arms crossed. It was a cool morning

but he wore a too-small singlet that emphasised his shoulders and biceps. Somehow his skin still held its tan from summer. Close up like this, Hesse saw his wiriness, the way his muscles seemed knotted to his bones. Jago flexed his hands when he talked like he was trying not to clench them into fists. Fists like the one that had collided with Hesse's cheekbone.

Jago reached across the board and slapped Hesse playfully on the back. 'Relax, bro. I just want to hire a board. I'm taking Fenna surfing this morning.'

Hesse looked up sharply. The passenger door opened, and Fenna stepped out. She leaned against the side panel, looked sheepishly at Hesse and gave him a little wave.

'Aunty Julie thought it'd be a good idea if Fenna got a lesson from someone a bit more experienced,' Jago said. Hesse had no idea Jago was related to the Turners.

Fenna looked at her feet and scuffed the gravel with the toe of her runners. She was dressed differently today, in a pair of skinny jeans and a long-sleeved T-shirt that stretched tight across her chest. Her hair was pulled back off her face and she'd hidden her freckles under make-up. She looked five years older.

'So,' Jago continued, 'we need to hire a foamy and a wetsuit.'

'We don't hire wetsuits,' Hesse said, defensively.

'Then we'll just have to buy one, won't we?' Jago said, smiling back at Fenna.

'No, really,' she began, but he held his palm up to her.

'Call it a welcome-to-Australia gift,' he said.

She winced but she couldn't look at Hesse.

'So, let's see what you've got inside,' Jago said to Hesse.

'Theo's in there. He'll help you.'

'Come on then, Fen. Let's get you fitted out.'

It was the first time Hesse had heard her name shortened. It didn't suit her.

Hesse stood with his hands on the deck of the board. He wanted her to look at him, to explain what she was doing with a dickhead like Jago, but she turned and followed the dickhead into the shop.

A few minutes passed before Theo stuck his head around the corner, the phone pressed against his chest. 'Hesse, could you look after these two? I'm on hold here.'

Hesse took his time, balling the wax from the board into a tight wad, daring himself to smear it on the windscreen of Jago's car. Finally, knowing what a barrage he would cop if he so much as touched the ute, he walked into the shop.

Fenna was in the fitting room at the back. The curtain wasn't fully closed, and Hesse saw Jago pretending not to look.

'How's that one, Fen?' he asked. She stepped out wearing a full-length steamer. It fitted her perfectly, so much better than Imogen's had.

'What do you think, Hesse?'

'Hesse isn't paying for it,' Jago said. 'But I think it looks great.'

'Yeah, it's a good fit,' Hesse agreed. 'Swing your arms a bit.'

She wiggled about and rolled her shoulders. Then she looked at the price tag on the sleeve. 'It's too much,' she said.

Jago already had his wallet out. 'Like I said, it's a gift.'

Fenna slipped behind the curtain as Jago swaggered over

to the counter. He beckoned Hesse with his finger, bringing his mouth close to his ear. 'She's out of your league, bro,' he said, unable to keep the smugness from his voice. 'She's not interested in schoolboys. She wants a man with some money to splash. And a car.' He slapped his credit card onto the counter.

When Fenna had finished dressing, Jago threw her the keys. 'Wait in the car, babe,' he said. 'I've got this.'

She shot a glance at Hesse then disappeared out the door.

Theo finished his call. 'I'll look after Jago,' he said to Hesse. 'You can get back to stripping that board.'

As Hesse walked outside, he heard Theo say, 'We've been having a few problems with the EFTPOS machine. It might take a while to warm up.'

Fenna was sitting on the bonnet holding her new wetsuit. She had pulled her hair out and it spilled onto her shoulders. 'I'm sorry,' she said before Hesse could say anything. 'You said I should meet more people.'

'Yeah, but Jago? Really?' Hesse turned into the stripping bay and picked up the scraper.

'He's not as bad as you think,' Fenna said, defensively. 'And besides, it's not like you and I are—'

'Yeew,' Jago called, marching towards his car. 'Let's go surfing!' He dropped the foamy into the back and opened Fenna's door for her. She slid into the seat without looking at Hesse, the tinted windscreen hiding her again.

Jago winked at Hesse. 'You have a good day,' he said, climbing in the driver's side. Once out on the road, Jago accelerated heavily and the back of the ute fishtailed. The horn blared as they disappeared around the corner.

Hesse went back to work on the board, feeling like the kid he was. It'd be years before he could afford a car. Most of the money he earned at the surf shop went towards his phone plan and school lunches. Plus, he was eyeing off a new board—a big gun he'd need to surf Razors. He hadn't told his mum, but ever since he'd seen the reef breaking on a big swell last winter, he'd thought about what it would be like to ride it. He hadn't even told Theo.

The day dragged. Business was slow compared to previous weekends, a few browsers but not many buyers. Theo went for his second coffee at twelve, leaving Hesse with two more consignment boards to clean. Once he'd stripped the decks, he sanded them, checked for dings and prepared some resin to fill them. Even masked up, the smell of the resin was strong enough to make him lightheaded. There was something about it that triggered good memories—his dad working on a board in the back shed, Hesse looking up at him from the bench seat by the door, his mum scolding his dad for allowing him in the shed with the fumes.

It was early afternoon when Jago's ute turned into the car park again and stopped side-on to Hesse. Without a word, Jago jumped out, took the foamy from the back and dropped it on the grass next to the stripping bay.

Hesse could see through the open car door. The front seat was empty. 'How'd you go?' he asked Jago.

'Awesome,' he replied. 'But listen, can I get a refund on this?' He reached into the front seat and held the wetsuit up for Hesse to see. It was dry and the tags were still attached.

'What happened?' Hesse asked.

'Nothin'. I just want a refund, that's all.'

'Where's Fenna?'

'Stuffed if I know. Now, that refund.'

'You'll have to talk to Theo.'

Jago walked off, leaving Hesse to wonder whether he should be happy their surf lesson hadn't worked out, or worried about Fenna.

His phone buzzed in his pocket. Fenna. *What time do you finish work?*

Jago was inside negotiating with Theo for a while. Eventually he returned to his car, slammed the door and drove off without another word.

Theo came outside just as Hesse was texting Fenna. 'Slacking off again, I see,' he said.

Hesse didn't bite. 'Did he say what happened?' he asked.

'Not a word. Fenna wasn't with him?'

'No, but she's just texted me.'

'She okay?'

'Dunno. She wants to meet after work.'

Theo had a habit of tugging on his beard when he was thinking. Hesse reckoned it was all for show—usually he'd already decided what he was going to say, and he just wanted to look like he'd thought it through. 'It's a slow day,' he said. 'Why don't you finish up now?'

Hesse had mended and sanded the last board. He ran his hand over the rail where he'd repaired it.

'Go on. Get going before I change my mind,' Theo said.

When Hesse pulled his daypack from behind the counter the wetsuit Jago had returned was stuffed inside.

Theo was behind him. 'It was a good fit,' he said.

'Awesome. Thanks, Theo. She'll love it,' Hesse replied.

He had texted Fenna to meet at the boatshed on the river. It was the regular meeting spot for kids in Shelbourne. A sheet of corrugated iron on the back wall had been prised loose years ago and was easily pushed aside. No one knew who owned the shed and there hadn't been boats in there for as long as Hesse could remember. Kids had fitted it out with an old mattress and a few chairs. It was damp inside and everyone knew to sit the mattress up on the chairs when they'd finished with it.

Fenna was waiting when he arrived. She'd changed into her regular cut-off shorts, tights and hoodie. She'd also wiped her face clean of make-up. '*Hai*,' she said as Hesse rolled his bike to a stop.

He wasn't sure what to expect. She'd all but ignored him when she came to the shop with Jago. 'How did the surf go?' he asked, leaning the bike against a tree.

'Sit down,' she said, patting the seat on the side of the shed protected from the wind. A weak sun had warmed the wall they leaned against. The cold front predicted for the afternoon hadn't arrived yet, but heavy clouds were building in the west.

Fenna looked out over the water. Hesse was close enough to see the deep ringlets of her hair, darker at the roots but lighter at the tips. 'So,' he said. 'What happened?'

'It was stupid,' she said. 'I never should have gone with him.'

'He didn't try anything?'

'No. I just didn't feel comfortable. I told him I needed to pee. And I ran.'

'You ran back from Corrals?'

'No. We were at a different beach, not so far.'

'Boneyards, most likely. There's no surf there anyway. Did he follow you?'

'I don't think so. He was probably more confused than anything. I'll have to apologise to him. I do such stupid things, Hesse. What's wrong with me?' She dug her elbows into her thighs and covered her face with her hands.

Hesse tentatively put his arm around her shoulder. He felt her tense and then soften as she leaned closer, slowly dropping her hands from her face. This friendship was getting more complicated by the day but still he was drawn to her.

'So,' he said, trying to shift the mood. 'It's a shame about that wetsuit. It was a great fit.'

She shrugged. 'Your mum's one fits me. Almost.'

He freed his arms, unzipped the daypack at his feet and pulled the wetsuit out.

Her eyes widened. 'No,' she said. 'I can't.'

'You can.'

'It's too much. Please, take it back.'

'It's not from me. It's from Theo.'

She stood and held the wetsuit in front of her, smiling and leaning towards him. Hesse slid his thumbs through the belt loops on her shorts, drawing her closer. Little strands of her hair flew in the breeze and caught in her mouth. She brushed them away and kissed him.

Eventually she sat down and they talked until the wind started to bite. The river turned to whitecaps and the tea trees whipped against the side of the shed.

'Will you be at school this week?' he asked.

She didn't answer for a while. 'I can't put it off forever, I guess,' she said quietly.

'There's no assembly on Monday morning, just some Literacy Week thing where we all have to read for half an hour in home room. It might get you used to the place a bit before—'

'Before I have to speak to the whole school.' Her body stiffened. 'Honestly, I don't think I can do that. I'll have a panic attack, I know it.'

'Well, you're not alone. Oliver and Ruby want me to speak at the forum next weekend.'

She didn't seem surprised. 'Are you going to do it?'

'I'm not sure.'

'You definitely should. You'd be great. I could help you write your speech.'

'Would you?'

'*Ja*, of course. Writing, I like. Talking, not so much.'

'Would you come to the meeting?'

'I wouldn't miss it.'

He liked the idea of having Fenna there. And the way he felt at the moment he'd give a speech at the United Nations if it meant she'd help him prepare it.

'I have to go,' she said.

'Yeah, me too.'

It was cold now. The wind cut right through Hesse's T-shirt. Fenna held the bundled wetsuit to her chest.

'Can you keep this at your place?' she asked, handing it back to him.

'Okay, but what if—?

'No,' she interrupted, 'I'm only going surfing with you from now on.'

They both stood up. It was more awkward without the easy contact of leaning into each other on the bench. He swayed forward and kissed her, their lips barely touching.

'See you tomorrow?' he said.

She shook her head. 'The Turners are taking me for a drive along the coast.'

'You'll like it,' he said. 'It's beautiful.'

She nodded.

'You've got my number,' he said.

'And you've got mine.' She took a couple of steps backwards.

'Is this the way you say goodbye in the Netherlands?' Hesse said walking backwards too.

She laughed. '*Ja*, it's an old custom. Very old.'

'See,' he said, 'this whole cultural exchange thing is working already. I'm learning so much.'

'Me too. Freezing my tits off. Shit hitting the fan.'

They were ten metres apart now. 'I'm thinking of becoming a cultural ambassador,' he said, having to raise his voice above the wind.

'You'd be good,' she called, continuing to move away. 'You'd have to learn to dance though.'

He threw in a couple of steps of the footy club shuffle.

She laughed. 'We really have some work to do on that. I might run a workshop.'

They were twenty metres apart. 'I don't know your last name,' Hesse called.

'De Vries.'

'I think I like you, Fenna De Vries.'

A smile lit her face. She waved, turned and headed across the playground towards the road. Hesse watched until she disappeared through the trees on the other side.

9

The rest of the weekend was taken up with homework, another quiet day at the surf shop and a house full of people on Sunday night as the planning for the community forum took shape. Twenty people spread through the lounge room and kitchen. Hesse spent most of the evening in his room, but Oliver spied him when he came out for a break and asked if he'd given any more thought to speaking at the meeting.

'Yeah, I'll do it,' he said. 'But I want to write it myself.'

Oliver shook Hesse's hand. 'Excellent,' he said.

Imogen was sitting at the kitchen table. 'You'll be great,' she said.

'Listen up, everybody,' Oliver said in his courtroom voice. 'Young Hesse is going to speak at the forum.'

They cheered. Hesse knew he was in deep now.

Ruby called for everyone's attention. 'This is a good opportunity to update you all on what's been happening and what to expect at the forum,' she said.

Hesse still had a stack of homework to finish, but he stopped to listen.

'First, thanks to the letter-writing group,' Ruby said. 'We got two letters in *The Chronicle* last week.'

There was a little round of applause.

'We need to keep the pressure on,' she continued. 'The publicity group has got posters ready to go up around town this week. If shop owners are reluctant to display them just emphasise it's a forum, it's not a protest meeting. We've got more actions planned for after the weekend, but for now I'll hand you over to Oliver.'

Oliver wore a pastel pink polo shirt and a pair of chinos. His attempt at a casual look was undermined by the fact he'd tucked the shirt into his pants. 'Thanks, Ruby,' he said. 'Can I start by asking how many of you are on Twitter?'

Half a dozen people raised their hands.

Others around the room tapped at their phones, most poking with one finger. Hesse reckoned he could guess a person's age by how many fingers they used on their phone.

'What about making a banner?' Eliza Wadsworth asked.

'Excellent idea,' Ruby cut in. 'It would be great to have one to put up in the hall on Sunday.'

'The thing is,' Oliver continued, 'the dominoes are falling into place for us. Climate change is everywhere in the media at the moment.'

'And right in the middle of all this,' Ruby said, 'Hadron is trying to quietly sell off one of the dirtiest and most polluting power stations in the country.'

Hesse was already making mental notes about what he might include in his speech and wondered what sea-level rise would mean for a town like Shelbourne. There were lots of houses close to the water out near Wangim Point, and more on the river flats.

Eventually, his brain had absorbed as much information as it could for one night, and he returned to his room. He checked his phone. There were the usual posts from his mates—dumb videos and clips of massive surf in Portugal—but nothing from Fenna.

Monday was cold. The wind had picked up overnight and Hesse had woken to the clatter of rain on the iron roof. Imogen was on day shift and was gone by the time he got up. He scoffed a quick breakfast and headed for the bus stop, sprinting between the shelter of overhanging trees along the river, but still ending up wet.

Everyone was huddled under the newsagency awning, trying to find some protection from the rain. Mus wore a beanie, a scarf and a heavy woollen overcoat that made him look like a mafia boss. Jake hopped from one foot to the other, willing his big frame to warm itself. Felicity sat in the comfort of her father's car. Fenna wasn't there.

Browny mounted the kerb before rolling off again and

bringing the bus to a stop with a hiss of air brakes.

'We really should tell the cops before he kills someone,' Tina said to no one in particular.

The kids bottlenecked at the door. Eventually they boarded, dropping their bags and pushing them under the seats. The bus was about to move off when Fenna appeared at the closed door.

Browny opened it. 'And who are you?' he asked, as she stepped up.

Fenna didn't reply. Her eyes flicked around the bus until she saw Hesse. She looked different in the uniform of grey pants, puke-green jumper and white shirt.

'You'll need a bus pass,' Browny said.

Hesse made his way to the front. 'Fenna's new, Browny. Exchange student from the Netherlands. She'll get a pass organised today.'

'All right, then. On ya get.'

Fenna followed Hesse down the aisle to the back of the bus, trying to ignore the stares and whispers. Hesse shepherded her into a vacant seat and sat next to her.

'What sort of cheese would you use to hide a horse?' Browny called, swinging around in his seat.

No one replied.

'Mascarpone!'

'Shit,' Tina said. 'His jokes are getting worse.'

Fenna sat low in her seat. She reached for Hesse's hand and put it on her wrist. Her pulse was racing. He squeezed her arm.

A large hand appeared from behind them. 'My name is Jacob. I am very pleased to make your acquaintance.'

Hesse smiled. 'This is Jake,' he said. 'And somewhere inside the coat next to him is Mus.'

Fenna sat up and turned around. 'I'm Fenna,' she said.

Both boys shook her hand. 'We know,' Mus said. 'Hesse has told us about you.'

Tina leaned over the aisle. 'You don't play footy, do you? You look fit. We need a full forward.'

Fenna's eyes widened, and Hesse explained. 'Aussie Rules,' he said. 'Tina's a gun.'

'Sorry,' Fenna said. 'I'm a swimmer back home. And a skater.'

'Ice skating,' Hesse cut in.

'If this weather gets any colder, you'll be able to skate to school,' Mus said.

Fenna gave him the briefest of smiles.

Felicity was keeping to herself. She offered Fenna a quick nod and turned away.

The conversation bounced around the back seats most of the way into Castlereagh. Fenna did her best to answer the onslaught of questions.

'How long are you here for?'

'How come you've arrived in May?'

'Is weed really legal in the Netherlands?'

'Where are your clogs?'

She answered politely until Hesse intervened. 'Okay, ease up,' he said.

Fenna sat back, her shoulder just touching Hesse's.

'Nice uniform,' he said, dryly.

She looked at him, trying to work out whether he was joking

or not. 'I've never worn a uniform in my life,' she said.

When they arrived at school, Fenna stuck close to Hesse. The day began in home room with half an hour of reading, but Fenna was called out to Mrs Shawshank's office. Hesse didn't see her again until recess. 'How'd you go with Shanky?'

'The principal?'

'Yeah, sorry,' he said. 'Everyone's got a nickname. You'll have one by the end of the day. Probably something really original, like cheesehead or cloggie.'

'She tried to be nice,' Fenna said, as they walked along the bustling corridor towards the canteen. 'But I have to come to school every day from now on or I could be sent home.'

The line at the canteen was more like a rugby scrum or a pack of hyenas trying to get at the carcass of a wildebeest. The canteen servers did their best to fill the students with sugar, salt and fat before they returned to class, where they learned about the obesity epidemic and type 2 diabetes. The Student Council had managed to get salads and sushi added to the menu, but the biggest sellers were still sausage rolls, chips, hot dogs and soft drinks.

Hesse was starving. He was always starving. Breakfast had been three hours ago, and he had to make it through double English with Dalgety before he could eat again. Getting served was more a matter of holding your ground in the melee than pushing and shoving. Hesse worked his way to the front, only to find himself directly behind Felicity Holden. For someone new to the school, her canteen game was pretty strong. When she was handed her order of chips and a fruit juice, she turned and bumped into Hesse and smiled. Her perfect teeth reminded him he hadn't been to the dentist in two years.

'Careful,' she said, her mouth close to his ear. 'Your girlfriend might get jealous.' She pushed against him a little harder than she needed to as she made her way out of the scrum. She said something to Fenna in passing, then disappeared around the corner.

Hesse was flustered and momentarily forgot his order but gathered himself and asked for two sausage rolls and a cup of soup.

'Sorry, luv,' the woman behind the counter said. 'There's been a run on the soup.'

He moved sideways to clear air and handed one of the sausage rolls to Fenna. She looked inside the bag with a mixture of curiosity and horror.

'It's okay,' he reassured her, pretending to read off the side of the bag. 'No animals were harmed in the making of this product.'

'They didn't have any *bitterballen*, then?' she asked, half smiling.

He shook his head, wondering what she was talking about.

'They're the best,' she said. 'Deep-fried balls with meat or vegetables. Great with beer.'

'Shit,' he said, turning back towards the canteen. 'I forgot the beer.'

She almost laughed.

'What did Felicity Holden say to you?' he asked.

'The blonde girl from the bus? The one you couldn't take your eyes off?'

Hesse blushed.

'She said, "Welcome to the jungle".'

'Oh, now that's a song you have to hear,' Hesse said. 'Tash Sultana.'

'Yes!' she said and surprised him by singing the opening lines. 'She's huge in Europe.'

There was a large undercover area that was really just a roof connecting two wings of the school. The wind whistled through but at least it kept the rain out. Artificial grass had been laid and tables with bench seats made from recycled timbers by VCAL students were scattered through the area. Hesse and Fenna found an empty table. It was hard not to be aware of other kids' looks. Fenna was the first exchange student at Castlereagh High since Tammy Whittaker, two years ago. Tammy was from Mississippi, and she went home pregnant.

'So, what else did Shanky have to say?' Hesse asked.

Fenna kept her head down, her hair veiling her face. Being stationary made her more conspicuous. 'I don't have to give a speech in front of the school straightaway,' Fenna said. 'Maybe just to the year elevens to start with.'

Mus and Jake came and sat with them. Jake had a plastic container with food from home, spicy-smelling meat and mixed beans in a salad. Mus didn't have anything. Hesse broke off a bit of his sausage roll and passed it to him. Fenna watched then did the same.

'Thanks,' Mus said. 'I love a mystery roll.'

'Mystery meat,' Hesse explained, laughing.

'I hear you're speaking at the forum on the weekend,' Jake said. 'I didn't know you were an expert on coalmining.'

Hesse hadn't been looking forward to this conversation. Jake's father, Ibrahim, drove one of the haul trucks that transported the coal from the open cut to the power station. It was well paid, and he'd been trained up to learn how to manoeuvre the massive truck in and out of the pit.

'I'm no expert,' Hesse began. He felt Fenna's foot touch his leg under the table. 'But they wanted a young person to speak. I'm going to talk about climate change mostly.'

Jake nodded. Hesse had been the first kid to hang out with Jake when his family had arrived two years ago. They had sat together on the bus and later that day Imogen had dropped around a lentil casserole. It's hard to imagine a place more remote from South Sudan than Shelbourne.

'So, do you think our mine and power station are going to have any effect at all on climate change? I mean, compared to what's happening in China and India,' Jake said.

'We've got to start somewhere,' Hesse said, biting into his sausage roll.

'You know if they can't find a buyer, Hadron may close? And my father won't have a job,' Jake said.

Hesse looked at his friend. It would be so much easier if he didn't know anyone who worked at Hadron. If the mine and power station closed he supposed Felicity's father would be transferred somewhere else, another mine in another community. Management skills were always needed. Less so coal-truck drivers.

'Sorry, mate,' he said, and he meant it.

They finished eating in silence. Mus picked at the flaky crumbs caught in his scarf. Jake used a plastic fork to stab at his food. Hesse kept his eyes on the table in front of him.

Recess ended with classical music over the PA. The school had abandoned bells in the hope students would be soothed by the music and arrive at class more chilled and ready to learn.

Dalgety's class was given over to watching *Romeo and Juliet*, with Leonardo De Caprio and Clare Danes. They'd begun studying the play the previous week and showing the film was Dalgety's admission of defeat in his quest to get the class to actually read it. At least this way they'd have some idea of the characters and storyline.

Fenna sat next to Hesse. 'I love this film,' she whispered.

Hesse felt the eyes of the class on them. The girls looked at Fenna, trying to figure her out. To him she didn't appear particularly different from them, but Hesse could see how she might seem aloof, sticking close to him and not saying much. And the boys looked at Hesse in a new way—the gangly surfer kid who seemed to have the undivided attention of the new Dutch girl.

At lunchtime, Hesse gave Fenna a tour of the school, ending in the library. Mrs Costanzo, the librarian, gushed over her and asked what books she liked reading.

'Mostly Dutch ones,' Fenna said.

Mrs Costanzo's smile slipped momentarily. 'I'm not sure we have any Dutch books,' she said. 'Maybe we could order some in.'

Mrs Costanzo ruled her library—and it was *her* library—like a queen constantly worried about being dethroned. In her column in the parent newsletter she was always banging on about her library being the beehive at the centre of a garden.

Hesse and Fenna moved between the shelves. At the end of a row, hemmed in by soft furniture, Felicity sat on the floor with her back to the wall. Her legs were tucked up and her head rested on her knees. A copy of *Romeo and Juliet* lay on the carpet next to her bag. She looked up abruptly, sensing Hesse and Fenna standing above her. Her eyes were rimmed red and she looked away immediately.

Fenna squatted down. 'Are you okay?' she asked, reaching out to put her hand on Felicity's knee. Maybe it was the quietness of the library, or the tension Hesse felt in the air, but her accent seemed stronger.

Felicity's face softened for an instant and she looked like she was about to say something. Then she hurriedly gathered her gear and got to her feet. 'I'm fine, thank you,' she said, pushing past Hesse. At the other end of the row, she turned. 'Shakespeare,' she said, trying to sound casual. 'He's so moving.'

On the bus on the way home Fenna sat with Hesse, Mus and Jake. She scrolled through her phone looking at Instagram and replying to messages. Hesse realised he'd never asked her about her friends back home.

'You're quiet,' he said to her.

She glanced at him. 'Just tired,' she replied, returning to her phone.

When they arrived in Shelbourne, Fenna said a quick goodbye and turned to walk towards home.

'Are you still going to help with my speech?' Hesse asked after her.

'Not tonight,' she said over her shoulder.

'No problem,' he said, hiding his disappointment behind a smile.

If she noticed, she didn't show it. She waved and disappeared around the corner by the pub.

'Are you really going to speak at that meeting?' It was Felicity. She stood next to him with her bag hitched onto her shoulder so her shirt and jumper lifted on one side showing a line of tanned skin.

'Yeah,' he said. 'I am.'

'You know Hadron will have people there? It won't just be greenies you'll be talking to.'

'*Greenies?*' he said. 'What is this, 1980?'

'You know what I mean.'

He looked directly at her then. There was something different in her eyes, in the tone of her voice. He wondered if it was concern but he dismissed the thought immediately. This was Felicity Holden, daughter of the Hadron manager, a refugee from Hastings Girls who'd always looked down on the kids she was now forced to call her classmates.

'It's just a forum. It's meant to start a discussion, that's all,' he said.

'I've seen your group's Twitter posts. "Shut It Down" doesn't sound like a discussion.'

'Yeah,' he said. 'The aim of the campaign is to block the sale and force Hadron to close. Whether that happens now or sometime in the future, it's going to happen. The whole place is old and rundown.'

'A stranded asset,' she said. 'That's what Dad calls it.'

He'd never had a conversation with Felicity like this before. Other than their argument in class he'd hardly spoken to her.

'What does that mean?' he asked.

She dropped her bag to the ground and crossed her arms. The wind had dropped during the day and the rain had cleared, but it was still cool. 'Well,' she said, 'Hadron wants to sell so it won't have to pay to rehabilitate the mine when it eventually closes. If they can't sell, it's a stranded asset. A liability. Your little group can jump up and down and have your market stalls and make your banners, but this'll be decided by economics. That's the facts of it.'

Hesse thought back to Oliver's speech about pressuring banks and shareholders. 'And what if we can influence the economics?' he said.

'A tiny group of'—she made air quotes with her fingers—'*concerned residents*. How are you going to influence the economics of a multinational company?'

'You'll just have to wait and see, won't you,' Hesse said. He knew he sounded pissweak.

She smiled. Genuinely. 'I admire your commitment,' she said. 'But you know your campaign is doomed to fail. Shelbourne is just one tiny cog in the machine. You mean nothing to Hadron.'

'Yeah, but if one tiny cog breaks—'

Just then her father's four-wheel drive nudged into the car park next to where they were standing. Terry Holden waved to his daughter.

'Gotta go,' Felicity said, picking up her bag.

Hesse realised he'd fallen comfortably into this conversation with her. It was uncharted territory for both of them. He felt he needed to finish on a friendly note.

'You should walk more,' he said, nodding his head towards the car. 'Keep fit.'

She pursed her lips and, for the briefest instant, poked her tongue out at him. He watched as she stepped up into the car, somehow managing to make it look graceful. Her father leaned towards her and they spoke briefly. Then he waved at Hesse. Hesse responded by lifting his chin and dropping it again.

Felicity drew the seatbelt across her chest. She might have smiled at Hesse, but with the windscreen between them it was hard to be sure.

10

The rain had exhausted itself during the day and the dull scent of tea trees and damp grass hung in the air. Hesse needed some space to think and he knew exactly where he could find it. He picked up his pace as he walked up the Russell Street hill to his front gate. Imogen would be home from work soon and he knew she'd hassle him about getting his homework done, so best to keep moving. He hacked off two slices of bread in the kitchen, spread them with butter and honey and scoffed them down. Then he changed and grabbed his wetsuit and bike from the shed.

Five minutes later, he was weaving his way through the sleepy Monday side streets, eventually emerging onto Ocean Road opposite the surf lifesaving club. He crossed the car park to the roller door at the front of the building. Skegs sat in his usual position, just inside the door, with a bundle of rope at his feet, his gnarled hands working to loosen knots in its length.

'Young Temps,' he said, looking up. 'Haven't seen you in a while.'

Skegs—Hesse never knew him by any other name—must have been in his seventies. His skin was like old leather and his joints were stiffened by salt and arthritis. He always smelled of Goanna oil. He lived in a small flat at the back of the club and looked after the gear in the garages. Anytime, any season, he'd be there, scuttling around like a crab. His inventory of the equipment, pretty much kept inside his head, was legendary. He knew when every rescue boat, every board, every piece of rope was bought and when it was last used, tested or serviced.

'Hey, Skegs,' Hesse said.

'Not much out there today,' he replied. 'Guess that's why you're not surfing. What're you after?'

'Just a paddleboard. Figured I'd head out to the point and back. Keep my fitness up.'

Skegs' life was the sea. He swam all year round and could still handle a surf ski in a reasonable swell. He knew Shelbourne beach like other people knew their families. And he held a place in his heart for anyone who shared his love of the ocean.

'Good lad,' he said, carefully placing the rope on the bench next to his seat. 'Water temperature's still good. About sixteen, I reckon. It's late in the season though. Should be colder by now.'

Hesse knew Swellnet was saying fourteen degrees, but he'd accept Skegs' rating over some distant website any day.

'You into your four-three yet?' Skegs asked.

This was part of the language of the coast, gauging the seasons by the thickness of wetsuit you wore.

'Nah, still in the three-two,' Hesse said. 'If I get into the four-three too early, it gives me nowhere to go when it gets really cold.'

Skegs smiled. 'Take number twenty-two,' he said, pointing at the closest yellow rescue board on the rack. 'It's a newy. Should glide through the water like a hot knife through butter.'

'Thanks,' Hesse said, sliding the board off the rack and carrying it out onto the grass at the front of the club. It had newly applied Hadron stickers along each side. He wondered if he'd get the same reception from Skegs after next weekend's forum. There'd be a lot of people taking sides on Sunday.

Hesse changed into his wetsuit and thanked Skegs again. He was halfway down the track to the beach when he heard the old man call. 'Hey,' he yelled, holding a fluorescent rash vest above his head. 'You know the rules.'

Skegs never let anyone borrow equipment without taking a vest as well. Hesse knew the old man would climb the rusted ladder to the tower with his binoculars every twenty minutes or so, to track his progress across the bay. He dropped the board in the sand and ran back to get the vest.

'It's quiet out there,' Skegs said. 'Still good practice to triangulate though, keep track of where you are. And the tide's on the turn. You taking the conveyor belt?'

'Yep,' Hesse said. 'Always.'

The conveyor belt was the permanent rip that ran along the

side of the rocky point immediately below the surf club. It was outside the flagged area when the beach was patrolled in the warmer months but someone in the tower always kept an eye on it. Summer brought tourists and backpackers to the coast, people with no idea about currents and shifting banks, let alone a rip that could drag them into deep water before they'd taken half a dozen strokes.

The water bit at Hesse as he drew the board into the shallows and slid onto the deck. It was always the same, making him doubt his choice of wetsuit until he found his rhythm and his muscles warmed to the paddling. Beyond the conveyor belt, the water deepened and changed colour as the sand-churned cloudiness of the rip gave way to the blue-green hue of the bay. Hesse fell into a steady stroke. The rescue boards were long and thick, designed for buoyancy and speed across the water.

After ten minutes, he eased off and sat up, straddling the board. Behind him he could just make out the figure of Skegs, leaning against the rail of the tower. He almost waved but he didn't want Skegs to think he was in trouble. To his right, the bay curved towards Wangim Point, a ribbon of sand below steep cliffs. Depending on the tide, it was a kilometre from the main beach to the point. A big low tide shortened the distance by a couple of hundred metres, but it was just past full now, so Hesse had plenty of water to work with.

He lay down again and paddled, lifting his head every minute or so to gauge his position. This was his happy place. Out here in the middle of the bay no one could hassle him or argue with him. He lifted his arms from the water and allowed the momentum of the board to carry him forward until it slowed and stopped. Once he checked his position again, he turned over and lay on his back, the vast sky above him, the depths of the bay below. The board rocked gently.

He closed his eyes and allowed the events of the last couple of weeks to wash over him: Fenna, the campaign, school, Felicity, the ongoing feud with Jago. Being out on the water gave him the chance to see his problems in a new light, like they were anchored to the land and he could view them from a distance. His breathing was easy, despite the exertion of the paddle out, and he opened his eyes to stare into the pale afternoon sky.

After a few minutes rest, he sat up to check he hadn't drifted in the current. He was halfway across the bay, and he still had a clear view of the tower. Seeking out the yacht club in the sheltered beach inside the point, then the tip of the rocks where the bay gave way to open ocean, he triangulated and guessed he'd drifted a little far inshore. Lying on his stomach again, he pointed the board a touch further east, and resumed paddling.

Before he realised it, he was within a hundred metres of the point. He had planned to sweep around in a wide arc and head directly back, but it was rare that the ocean was so calm and he wanted to take advantage of the conditions. The sun was low in the west behind him, but he still had an hour of daylight, and half an hour of twilight beyond that.

He'd only ever seen Razors from the shore. It was marked by masses of white water when big winter waves exploded across the shallow reef. It broke once the swell rose above three metres, closing out the beaches and turning the bay into a cauldron.

Only the bravest, or most stupid, surfers on the coast dared to take it on. They'd paddle out from the yacht club, protected by the point until they hit deeper water, exactly where Hesse now sat. Beyond the shelter of the point, they'd become specks in the distance, stroking over the top of feathering mountains of water, hoping not to get caught by a rogue wave that could ragdoll them across the reef and hold them under for up to a minute.

Now, though, the ocean was a mirror. The breeze had dropped completely, and there was barely a ripple of swell. Hesse took his bearings again. He knew if he kept the shade sails on the deck of the yacht club behind his right shoulder and made sure they didn't disappear behind the rocks of the point, he'd be heading directly for Razors. He was alert now, watchful. He had always been a slim build, but his arms and shoulders were strong from hundreds of hours of paddling. The rhythm took over again and he felt the smooth glide of the board under him. He was flying.

Today, the reef at Razors was nothing more than a darker patch on the deep green of the ocean, maybe fifty metres wide. Hesse steered the board in over the top of it and sat up, dangling his feet into the darkness below. He had always wondered if he might feel something out here, like some element of his dad could still exist in the water, in the kelp beds, in the rocks and barnacles that clung to the reef.

All Hesse's energy since he'd lost his dad had gone into trying to remember the good things about him, the times they had shared, the surfing and fishing and swimming. The jokes and laughter, the car trips and meals and video games. But over time the memories had begun to slip and he feared they would fade and disappear no matter how hard he tried to hang onto them.

He slid off the side of the board, took half a dozen breaths, blocked his nose and pushed air into his cheeks to equalise—and dived. The reef was largely hidden by kelp wafting in the current, but underneath the rock was criss-crossed with sharp ridges and pinnacles that could shred a wetsuit—and the skin inside it. Hesse held his position by sliding his hand into a small fissure and looked up at the silhouette of his board on the surface. His lungs were nearly empty, and he felt the pressure of the depth at his temples.

Had his dad been dragged across the reef here, cut and torn by the rocks that gave the break its name? Held under and screaming for breath, where had his mind taken him in those last seconds—to his wife, his ten-year-old son? Or had he been too panicked to think of anything other than finding the surface and pulling air into his lungs before the next wave took him down again?

Hesse knew instinctively there would be no answers for him on a placid day like this. If he was to understand anything about his dad's death, it'd be when the swell was double overhead and Razors was breaking wild and mean. And he'd have to be out here.

He pushed off the reef and resurfaced, gulped air and rested his elbows on the deck of the board. In the western sky, the sun fractured the clouds low to the horizon and set the water alight with an amber glow.

With the tide now an hour past high, the paddle back was slower. Fatigue tugged at Hesse's muscles, but he maintained a steady speed, heading for the surf club tower.

A light was still on in one open garage when Hesse carried the board back up the track to the clubhouse. Skegs stood in the doorway with a plate of food balanced in one hand, a fork in the other.

'You got a bit off course,' he said. 'Thought you were just going to the point and back.' There was something knowing in his voice.

'It was so nice out there,' Hesse responded. 'Decided to go a bit further.'

'Razors,' Skegs said, nodding.

'I hadn't been out that far before. Thought I'd have a squiz.' Hesse carefully lifted the board onto the rack then peeled off the rash vest and wetsuit. His clothes were dry and warm.

'He was a good bloke, your dad,' Skegs said, staring out into the gathering dark.

Hesse had his jumper halfway over his head. He stopped. He'd never spoken to Skegs about anything other than the beach, the ocean and the equipment.

He pulled the jumper on and came out to stand next to Skegs. 'Did you surf together?' he asked.

Skegs laughed. 'No. Back then clubbies and surfers didn't mix. We avoided each other.'

'So how did you know him?'

Skegs swept his hand around the inside of the garage. 'He was good with the tools. All those racks—he built them.'

119

Hesse looked more carefully at the rows of boards and skis. The racks were metal framed with timber supports covered with carpet to protect the equipment.

'I liked him,' Skegs continued. 'Damn shame, what happened.'

Hesse hesitated. 'Do you remember that day?'

'Everyone in Shelbourne remembers that day.'

Again, Hesse waited.

'It was a huge swell. Popped up out of nowhere. Swells like that usually take longer to build. You keep an eye on a big low-pressure system in the Bight,' he said waving vaguely towards the south. Remembering the plate of pasta in his hand, he dug his fork in and ate a couple of mouthfuls, before wiping his mouth with his sleeve. 'It peaked quickly and was mostly gone the next day.'

'Do you reckon Dad should have been out there?' Hesse asked. 'At Razors.'

'I can't answer that, mate. We put a rescue boat out in the dark, though. Dangerous as all hell in a swell like that, but we thought there was a chance we'd find him.'

'Were you on the boat?' Hesse asked.

'Yeah. Me, Theo and Bob Young.'

Hesse had never been told this. He looked at Skegs. The fluorescent light from the garage caught the grey stubble on his chin. He rocked slightly from side to side as though he might have been back on that boat, trying to stay alive while risking his life to help a lost surfer. Hesse waited for him to say more, but Skegs finished the last of his pasta and scraped the plate onto the grass.

'Thanks, Skegs,' Hesse said eventually, as the old man reached up to grab the roller door handle, pulling it down on another day.

'No problem, young fella.'

Fenna was already at the bus stop when Hesse arrived the following morning. She stood with her back to the window of the newsagency and her face hidden behind her hair. She pulled a bud from one ear and held it out for him. He leaned against the window and put the bud in his ear. It might have been the same band she'd danced to in his kitchen, but he couldn't be sure.

They sat together on the bus. Browny's dad joke—what's the difference between a buffalo and a bison? You can't wash your hands in a buffalo—had been met with groans and the shaking of heads. The windows fogged with the breath of twenty teenagers and the bus filled with the smell of damp clothes and Lynx. Hesse touched Fenna's hand. She passed him a secretive smile and threaded her fingers through his. Near them, Felicity had her head in a book, Mus was already asleep, his chin buried in his woollen scarf, Jake was lost in whatever music was playing through the enormous headphones he carried with him everywhere and Tina was busy rolling the cigarettes she'd smoke at recess and lunchtime.

When they arrived at school, they were surprised to hear an unscheduled assembly had been called. As they entered the gym Fenna veered off and disappeared into the toilets.

As everyone settled, Mrs Shawshank strode onto the small

stage, a woman on a mission. She dropped a sheaf of paper on the podium and spent a long time straightening it. Teachers worked the sides of the horde like sheepdogs, pushing reluctant students into the space at the front.

'Good morning,' Mrs Shawshank said. Her mouth was too close to the microphone so it buzzed and distorted.

Silence fell. On the way in Mus and Jake had been guessing at what might have happened. More graffiti on the locker-room walls? Kids in uniform behaving badly at the local shopping centre? Drugs? The possibilities were endless. Tina shoved mints into her mouth to disguise the smell of the cigarette she'd just smoked.

Shawshank looked impatient. She took a deep breath before beginning. 'Now, I know there are issues that we are all concerned about,' she began, 'and the state of the environment is something everyone—teachers, students, parents—takes very seriously. But this,' she brandished the papers in her hand and shook them, 'is not the way to go about sensible discussion. It's not the Castlereagh way.'

No one had ever heard an actual definition of the Castlereagh way. It seemed to be an idea that changed to suit whatever aspect of student behaviour Shanky didn't like.

Hesse recognised the pamphlets. They were the ones advertising the School Strike for Climate. There was one planned for Castlereagh next month and he was thinking of going.

'Yes,' Shawshank continued, 'climate change is a very real threat, but plastering posters around the school is not the way to respond. The civilised way, the Castlereagh way, is to write letters, even make an appointment to meet your local member with your parents. We have a government for a reason, and we need to trust it to do the right thing for the country.'

Murmurs of dissent spread around the assembly. Even some of the teachers looked uncomfortable.

'How long till she gets onto littering in the yard?' Tina whispered.

The principal was on a roll. 'The Education Department has been very clear on this issue. Any student—I repeat *any* student—who is not at school on the day of this strike without a doctor's certificate, will be suspended. No discussion, no negotiation.'

The murmuring grew louder.

'I admire your commitment,' Shawshank said, shooting death stares at the teachers who weren't supporting her in quietening the kids. 'But if you really want to do something about the environment, you could start by picking up your own rubbish in the yard.'

'Bingo!' Tina said, loudly.

Mr Thorpe, one of the deputy principals, pointed at her and beckoned her to the side of the hall. As Tina stood up, cheering broke out. Thorpe's head swivelled, but he was outnumbered, unable to discipline eight hundred kids at a time.

Shawshank waited, determined to maintain her authority. When the commotion eventually died down, a girl near the back stood up. It was Rachel Cheng. She was in year ten and the president of the Student Environment Council. Her nickname was Greta.

While the teachers closest to her told her to sit down, Rachel stayed standing.

'This is not the time for a discussion, Rachel,' Shawshank said eventually. 'Now, please sit down.'

Mr Thorpe tried to move through the crowd to get to Rachel but the kids around her shuffled closer, blocking his path.

'The problem is,' Rachel said in a loud, clear voice, 'there never seems to be a right time to talk about climate change. And if the government *was* doing its job, we wouldn't have to go out on strike. But it's doing nothing, so it's up to us to force it to act. It's a climate emergency!'

This time the cheers were long and sustained.

Rachel raised a clenched fist in the air and yelled, 'Friday the twentieth! Join the Climate Strike. Eleven o'clock at the Town Hall.'

Two teachers, Thorpe and Mrs Carlson, had reached her by now, but they knew they couldn't touch her. She stood her ground while Thorpe did all the talking. The hall buzzed with tension.

Shawshank abruptly ended the assembly, instructing students to return to their home rooms. As a tactic to take the spotlight off the confrontation between Rachel and the teachers it worked. Hesse tried to get closer to Rachel to hear what the teachers were saying to her, but he was quickly shooed away. Tina had been forgotten in the commotion and took the opportunity to slip out of the hall.

Hesse, Mus, Jake and Tina walked back to their classroom together. Felicity tagged along behind. Fenna reappeared and fell in beside Hesse. He gave her a querying look, but she ignored him. When she spoke, they all turned to face her. 'We had the climate strikes in the Netherlands,' she said quietly. 'Everyone went.'

'I like the idea of a day off school,' Mus said. 'But I don't want to get suspended.'

'If enough people went,' Felicity said, 'they couldn't suspend everyone.'

'Woah,' Tina said. 'Don't tell me the coalminer's daughter has found her rebel heart.'

If they expected Felicity to arc up at this, she disappointed them.

'Your parents work at Hadron, too,' Felicity said, nodding at Jake and Tina. Tina seemed momentarily lost for words. 'It doesn't mean you have to think everything they think, does it?'

'What about all your arguments in Dalgety's class?' Mus said.

'I don't disagree with my dad,' Felicity continued. 'But I've got a voice of my own.'

'So, you'll be at the climate strike?' Mus asked.

'And get suspended'? Felicity scoffed. 'Not likely. Besides, it won't achieve anything. You all know that, right?'

'We've got to start somewhere,' Mus said defiantly.

'Sorry to break it to you, but a couple of hundred schoolkids in Castlereagh aren't going to change the world.'

'You know Greta Thunberg started out on her own?' Fenna said. 'One girl outside the Swedish parliament with a sign.'

'And good on her,' Felicity said, barely hiding the sarcasm in her voice. 'But she doesn't hold any power. Governments pretend to listen to her then they go back to business as usual. It's all about the money.'

Hesse waited for Fenna's response. He hadn't seen her challenged like this before. In fact, he'd hardly heard her speak in front of the others.

'It depends on what sort of power you're talking about,' she said.

'The power to actually change things. The sort of power governments have,' Felicity replied.

Fenna thought about that for a few seconds. 'But you just said governments go back to business as usual. So, they don't ever really change anything—they just keep doing what they've always done. That's why we need another way.' She stood her ground in front of Felicity. 'Don't you see?' she continued, her voice rising. 'We're the last generation. It's got to be us. If we don't act, it'll be too late.'

Felicity shook her head. 'Everyone will say how committed you are, but they know you don't vote, and you don't spend enough money. So, you won't change anything.'

'That's so defeatist,' Hesse said.

'What do you think you're going to change in Shelbourne on the weekend, Hesse?' Felicity said. 'Nothing—that's what. I wish you luck, I really do, but Hadron will crush your little group of activists and turn the whole town against you. You're going to make enemies you don't even know exist.'

'What do you mean by that?' Hesse asked.

'You'll see,' she said, and walked away towards their home room.

11

Having made the decision to speak at the forum, it seemed to Hesse the long weekend arrived at warp speed. Sunday dawned ominously cold and wet. Theo had given him the day off, but Hesse was awake early anyway, running through his speech in his head. Rain beat on the iron roof and the house shook when thunder clapped overhead. He pulled the doona under his chin and considered the day ahead.

He'd worked on the speech all week, fretted about it and shown no one other than Fenna. She'd come for dinner twice and helped him organise his thoughts and get them on paper. He still had no idea whether it was any good or how it would be received. Oliver had given him some tips on presentation—how to project his voice, keep his chest open and not rush—most of which he knew from the debating team he'd been part of in junior school. Fenna said she'd sit at the back so he could focus on her. For all their tips and support, he regretted agreeing to speak and wondered if there was still time to back out, find an excuse, lose his voice at the last minute. People would understand.

Imogen and Bear were sitting at the kitchen table with cups of coffee. The smell of the stovetop espresso filled the air. They both sprang to attention when Hesse came down the hallway. Bear had arrived late last night, after his shift at the pub. Hesse looked through the concertina doors to the lounge room, checking to see if anyone had slept on the couch. Nothing. No rumpled blankets, no pillow.

'Good morning, sunshine,' Imogen said, a little too chirpily.

Hesse eyed them, enjoying their discomfort. He really didn't care if Bear and Imogen were sleeping together. Though he hadn't considered what it might mean for him. Bear worked odd hours and Imogen was tied to her shifts at the hospital. Hesse liked his time alone but, at least for now, Bear would probably only be here when Imogen was home. He wasn't moving in; they were just seeing each other, though that phrase took on a whole new meaning now.

'Morning,' he replied, filling a bowl with Weet-Bix and sloshing milk over the top.

'All ready for today?' Bear asked.

'I guess I have to be,' Hesse said.

'You'll be fine.' Imogen leaned across the table and touched his arm. 'It's a brave thing, speaking in front of so many people. I'm so proud.'

'Ease up, Mum. I'm nervous enough as it is. Chances are, I'll stuff it up completely.'

'No way,' Bear said. 'You'll be awesome. And we'll be right there with you.'

It had been decided that Imogen would chair the forum and Bear would watch for trouble. If he stood up—all two metres of him—no one was going to argue. There were to be four speakers: Oliver, Ruby, Hesse and a woman from Friends of the Earth.

'Let's hope the weather improves,' Imogen said as another squall rattled the house. 'People won't come out if it keeps up like this.'

Hesse saw a positive side to the rain. Maybe no one would come. Maybe he'd be talking to a dozen people at most, just the Shelbourne Action members. Suddenly he wanted the rain to continue, to wash away any likelihood of a crowd.

His phone buzzed. A text from Fenna. *Hai. Freezing my tits off here. You?*

He laughed.

'Fenna?' Imogen asked.

He nodded.

Can you come over this morn? he replied.

Sorry. Going shopping with Julie. See you at the meeting.

'So,' Bear said. 'Bacon and eggs anyone?'

Hesse's mood brightened immediately. There were definite advantages to your mum's boyfriend being a chef. The quality of meals at the Templeton household was about to improve immeasurably. Imogen had never pushed her vegetarianism on Hesse and now the intoxicating smell of cooking bacon took over from the coffee. Bear boiled a pot of water, added vinegar and dropped eggs into it, swirling them to form moist little balls of white with the yoke encased inside.

The rain was coming in on a vicious south-westerly, whipping the trees against the side of the house and lifting a sheet of loose roofing iron. Bear looked at the ceiling. 'I'll fix that,' he said. Hesse and Imogen exchanged glances. Things were going to be a bit different around here.

His stomach filled with cereal, bacon, eggs and toast, Hesse returned to his room. It was still hours until the forum. He listened for a break in the rain, hoping he could get outside and clear his head. But if anything, the beating on the roof got heavier. He printed out his speech and went through it for the hundredth time, trying to picture Fenna sitting on his bed, offering suggestions as they'd worked on it on Thursday night. She had worn a pair of tight black jeans and a T-shirt with a surf logo on the front.

'So, you're a total surfer girl, now?' he'd joked.

She'd stood up on the bed and mimicked riding a wave, her arms spread wide.

'Your feet are too close together,' he'd said. 'And bring your arms in.'

Fenna had feigned wiping out. She dropped onto the bed and grabbed him. They laughed, rolling together from one side to the other.

Then she'd lain on top of him, the weight of her body on his, and their laughter had fallen away. She was so close he could feel her breath on his face. He'd run his hand up under her T-shirt, touching the silky softness of her skin, until he'd felt the strap of her bra.

'How's that speech going?' Imogen had called from the hallway.

'It's coming along,' Hesse had replied, trying to keep his voice even.

Fenna had slid off him and was sitting on the side of the bed, her hair a mess, when Imogen opened the door, carrying a tray with cups of hot chocolate and a plate of biscuits.

'Interesting way to be writing a speech,' Imogen said.

Hesse had jumped up and taken the tray. 'Awesome, Mum. Thanks.'

Now, the room seemed empty. In fact, anytime he wasn't with Fenna, something was missing. Maybe this was what being in love was like, this feeling of wanting to be with someone so much you felt hollow when they weren't there. It was the excitement of discovering someone new, someone he wanted to be with, even if they were doing nothing, even if they weren't talking. Like riding home on the bus, sitting next to each other, sharing earbuds. Or just watching her, the way she could raise one eyebrow on its own, her habit of moistening her lips with her tongue before she spoke.

The sound of voices in the kitchen brought him back to the present. When he walked out of his room he found Jake's parents, Ibrahim and Grace, unwrapping themselves from wet coats as Imogen pulled chairs out for them. Ibrahim was as tall as Jake and Grace wasn't much shorter. With Bear in the kitchen as well, they seemed to fill all the space.

Ibrahim shook Hesse's hand. They'd met a few times at Jake's place, though Hesse had seen more of Grace.

Bear offered them coffee. 'No, thank you,' Grace said, her voice polite but short.

Hesse began to worry something might have happened to Jake.

'What can we help you with?' Imogen asked. She was as confused as Hesse was about why they had come.

Ibrahim spread his large hands on the table. 'We wanted to talk to you before the meeting today,' he began.

Hesse felt the bacon and eggs rise uncomfortably in his stomach.

'You know I work at the mine,' Ibrahim continued.

'Yes, Hesse has told me,' Imogen said.

'But you want to block the sale—close the mine and the power station,' Ibrahim said. 'We don't understand why you would do this, why you would want to take away the jobs of so many people.'

'And you, Hesse,' Grace said. 'You are Jacob's friend. Why are you doing this to us?'

Hesse liked Grace. She had welcomed him into their home, fed him and joked with him about football and surfing. And Jake was one of his best mates.

Imogen sat back in her chair and looked briefly at Bear while Ibrahim and Grace waited. 'This is not directed at you, Ibrahim,' she said. 'I'm sorry your job has been placed in jeopardy, but we have been working for five years to make Hadron accountable for the environmental damage it has caused.'

'Damage?' Ibrahim interrupted. 'What damage?'

Hesse knew there was no easy way out of this conversation. Nothing he or Bear or Imogen could say would change anything for Jake's parents.

'We're not against you,' Hesse said. 'It's about Hadron and coalmining and climate change.'

'But Hadron *is* the workers,' Ibrahim responded. 'You must see that. What will I do if I lose my job? Where will we go?'

It was like Ibrahim and Imogen were speaking different languages.

'I beg you,' Grace said to Hesse. 'Please don't do this.'

Hesse looked to Imogen for help. She checked her watch. They'd promised to set up the hall for the meeting. 'I'm sorry,' she said, 'but we have to go.'

Ibrahim and Grace stayed seated, waiting for an answer Hesse and Imogen couldn't give them.

'Yes, of course,' Ibrahim said eventually. 'Thank you for your time.' There was a quiet dignity in his voice. He may have been angry and afraid of losing his job, but he would still be polite.

When they stood up to leave, Grace helped Ibrahim into his coat, and he did the same for her. They looked tired. Ibrahim shook their hands, Hesse first, then Imogen and, finally, Bear. Grace nodded her goodbyes and Imogen showed them to the front door. They left without another word.

Hesse and Bear waited at the table for Imogen to rejoin them.

'They've got a point,' Hesse said. 'And it's not just them. All the other families will be feeling the same.'

Imogen spoke firmly. 'Nothing like this ever happens without someone getting hurt, Hesse. It's the nature of change.'

'It's okay, Mum. I get it. It's just harder when you have to look at the people getting hurt every day.'

Imogen stood behind Hesse and rested her hands on his shoulders. 'You don't have to do it, Hesse. Not if it doesn't feel right.'

'I need some time to think,' he said.

'Okay. But you'll have to decide in time for Ruby and Oliver to organise another speaker,' Imogen said.

They drove the two blocks to the hall. The rain had eased slightly, but water lay in sheets across the bitumen car park. Tree debris was scattered everywhere and a large branch had fallen on the fence of an adjoining house. The wind cut straight through them as they ran from the car to the porch where Oliver, Ruby and half a dozen others were waiting. Imogen had the key and they squeezed into the small space, a nest of puffer jackets, as she unlocked the large front doors.

Ruby took Hesse's arm gently. 'All good?' she asked.

Hesse nodded.

'You'll be great,' Oliver said.

With Ruby on one side, Bear on the other, Imogen out front and Oliver behind, they swept him into the hall like some prince, like he was their key man, their advantage. But all the prince felt was his breakfast heavy and unsettling in his stomach.

For the next couple of hours, the hall was a hive of activity.

They set out more than a hundred chairs, Oliver reasoning they might as well err on the side of caution. 'Who knows how many we'll get,' he said. 'We don't want people standing for an hour and a half.' The rain didn't worry him. He still expected a big crowd.

Hesse convinced himself he wasn't putting off his decision, just thinking it over, but Imogen's not-so-subtle glances every few minutes reminded him time was running out.

Eliza Wadsworth and two women from the banner-making group arrived with ropes and ladders and a big roll of canvas. They spread it across the stage and raised it into position. Written in huge black letters on a white background were the words, SHUT IT DOWN. The I in the middle was a smokestack belching dark smoke into the sky and below it sat the hulking silhouette of the power station.

There was an audible intake of breath from almost everyone present.

'I think our forum just became a protest meeting,' Oliver said.

'Yep,' Imogen said. 'We've shown our hand now.'

Hesse wondered how people coming through the door that afternoon, expecting an information session, would react when they saw the banner blaring its message from the stage. It meant the meeting had the potential to be more hostile, filled with anger that could be directed at him as one of the speakers. They'd ask him awkward questions, interrupt him, howl him down.

Hesse opened the emergency-exit door and lurched out onto

the path along the side of the hall. The eaves protected him from the worst of the rain, but water overflowed from the spouting and hit his back as he doubled over and vomited in the garden. With his hands on his knees, he retched until it felt like there was nothing left inside him. He didn't know whether he felt better or worse. His stomach still churned but his head was lighter. He turned his face up to the rain and allowed it to cool him.

'Compliments to the chef?' Bear stood in the doorway, blocking the view of anyone in the hall. 'Waste of good bacon and eggs.'

Hesse grimaced. 'Sorry,' he said.

'You're just nervous. You'll be right,' Bear replied, handing him sheets of paper towel from the bathroom.

'Nervous?' Hesse said. 'I'm shitting myself.' He wiped his face and mouth and scrunched the towel in his hands.

'So, you're going to do it?'

Hesse pulled the cool, sweet air into his lungs. 'I'm still not sure. I don't want to let everyone down.'

'You know what I do when I have to make a tough decision?' Bear asked.

Hesse shook his head.

'I try to think of how I'll feel in a week, two weeks, a month. Whether I'll feel good about it or not.'

'So?'

'So how do you reckon you'll feel next week if you don't make the speech today?'

'Relieved,' Hesse said without thinking.

'Really?'

'Nah,' he reconsidered. 'I'd be disappointed I chickened out.'

Bear shrugged his enormous shoulders. 'There you have it, then.'

Hesse cupped his hands and caught some of the rain dripping from the spout. He splashed his face with it. 'Yep,' he said. 'There you have it.'

'Come on,' Bear said. 'We're finished setting up. Let's go home and rest up, find you some food you can hold down.'

'I might walk,' Hesse said.

Bear cast a sceptical eye at the sky but didn't argue with him. 'See you at home,' he said.

It didn't escape Hesse's attention that Bear had just called their place home.

Before he left the hall, Hesse found a quiet corner and pulled out his phone. The visit from Ibrahim and Grace was messing with his head. He understood how it must have hurt their pride to come and plead with him. The least he could do was to let Jake know he was going ahead with his speech.

Sorry mate, he texted, *but I've got to do this.*

He grabbed his puffer jacket from the rack by the front door and headed out into the car park. The south-westerly felt like it was coming straight off Antarctica, but the rain was light enough for him to walk without getting drenched. Hands deep in his pockets, he made his way down to Ocean Road before turning away from home, towards the surf shop. It would be a quiet day for Theo. Weather like this kept daytrippers away and any self-respecting surfer would have checked the wind this morning and gone straight back to bed.

Theo was in the shaping bay, putting the finishing touches on a blank before glassing it. His big hands stroked the rails gently with a square of sandpaper sitting neatly in his palm. 'Thought I gave you the day off,' he said, pulling the protective mask from his face.

Hesse shrugged. 'I just needed somewhere quiet to sit for a bit,' he said.

'Well,' Theo said, picking up the foam blank and holding the rail to his eye, checking the line, 'you've come to the right place. Haven't had a customer all morning.'

The shop was warm, and Hesse liked the way it closed in around him. The mix of smells—surf wax and incense and fibreglass resin—was comforting. He sat on the high stool in the corner of the shaping bay and watched Theo work. His grey hair was tied back, its bulk restrained under a beaten peak cap and his beard, pulled in by the customary rubber band, was stuffed into the top of his T-shirt.

'Today's the day, huh?' Theo said, his focus on the board. He flipped it over and used a square and rule to mark out the thin rectangles where the fin boxes would be cut into the blank. It was a big board—Hesse guessed at least seven-foot-six. A gun with volume to it and a shape that would give it speed on the open face of a wave.

'I don't know why I agreed to do it,' Hesse said, unzipping his jacket.

'You're doing it because you know you should,' Theo replied. 'I'm proud of you.'

'Not you too? Everyone's proud of me but I haven't done anything yet.'

Theo lifted the board off the padded rack and held it out to Hesse. 'What'd you reckon?' he asked.

Hesse hopped off the stool and took the board in his hands. It was light and smooth and still coated with fine foam dust. He ran his hands along the rail then turned it over to check the rocker, the slight curve from the middle of the board up to the nose. The dust coated his palms. 'It's beautiful,' he said.

Theo took it back and laid it on the rack again. He took a pencil and etched the dimensions into the blank, along the line of the stringer: *7'6" x 18¾" x 2½"*

He hesitated, then added *for Hesse.*

'What!' Hesse said.

'Reckon this will be your Razors board,' Theo said.

'But I can't afford it.'

'We can figure that out later.'

Theo straightened to his full height and pulled the beard from inside his T-shirt. The board lay between them and he rested his hands on it. 'I know you'll surf Razors at some stage, and you'll need the right board. But, also…' He hesitated.

Hesse waited.

'This arvo,' Theo said, finally. 'It's not easy, what you're doing. Giving that speech. You're putting yourself out there. People might try to tear you down. This is just, I dunno, a way of saying I've got your back.'

Hesse looked at Theo, this man who'd been his surrogate father since his dad died. He held his hand out for Theo to shake.

'None of that rubbish,' Theo said, walking around the rack and grabbing Hesse in a bear hug. The old man smelled of resin and coffee and his shirt was coated in dust. 'Now,' he said, holding Hesse at arm's length, 'you'd better get organised. You've got some serious shit-stirring to do.'

'You gonna be there?' Hesse asked.

'Wouldn't miss it.'

'Who'll look after the shop?'

'I hardly think there'll be a rush of customers this arvo. And if there is, stuff 'em. Some things are more important.'

12

The house was filled with people preparing for the forum. Oliver and Ruby had covered the kitchen table with their notes as they put together the running sheet with Imogen. She met Hesse's eye and nodded at him. Bear must have told her he'd decided to speak.

'Hey,' she said. 'This was on the front step when I got back.' She handed him a large orange envelope with his name on the front. Underneath it was series of numbers and letters that meant nothing to him: *tb756bnd$5#bd*

'You didn't see who left it?' he asked, turning it over in his hands.

'Nope,' she replied. 'I thought it might be something to do with school. Homework?' She went back to her notes.

Hesse opened the envelope. Inside were five A3 spreadsheets. The first column listed dates, with others across the page listing numbers. They meant nothing to him.

What he did recognise was the Hadron header at the top of each sheet.

'Any idea what these might be,' he said, putting them on the table.

'Where did they come from?' Oliver asked. He'd been too busy to hear Imogen's explanation earlier.

'I dunno. They were left on the doorstep.'

Oliver handed them to Ruby. 'Do these mean anything to you?' he asked.

Ruby was immediately seized by what she saw. She flicked through each sheet, checking them again and again. 'Unbelievable,' she said.

She had everyone's attention now and they crowded around the table.

'What are they?' Oliver asked.

'Air monitoring figures,' she replied. 'Specifically, sulphur dioxide. SO_2.'

'And...'

'And, they can't be right. They're off the charts.'

'What do you mean?' Imogen asked.

'These figures are way higher than WHO safe exposure levels,' Ruby said.

'But isn't all that information on the public record?' Oliver asked.

'Hadron self-monitors and reports directly to the regulators,'

Ruby said. 'But on these figures, they'd be shut down immediately. SO_2 is highly toxic in these concentrations.'

'I thought carbon dioxide was our main concern,' Imogen said.

Ruby shook her head. 'We've always known Shelbourne coal is high in sulphur. When they burn it in the power station, they're supposed to have filters to capture the SO_2 produced. If these figures are right, their filters aren't doing much.'

'Can we check the numbers against what Hadron has reported?' Oliver asked.

Ruby opened her laptop and started typing. 'Ah, of course,' she said after a minute. 'Because they self-regulate, all their data is held in confidence, which means we'd have to go through Freedom of Information to get at them. That could take months.'

'What about the Hadron website?' Bear asked.

'We wouldn't get past their firewall,' Ruby replied.

'So, we have no way to verify the figures,' Oliver said. 'Meaning we can't use them.' He sounded deflated after the initial excitement of Ruby's revelations.

'And the meeting starts in an hour,' Imogen added.

'That firewall,' Hesse said. 'You'd need a password?'

'Yes,' Ruby responded.

Hesse placed the envelope on the table. 'Could this be it?' he asked, pointing at the list of random letters and numbers written on the front.

Ruby brought up the Hadron website and entered the password.

Everyone held their breath as she clicked the log-in button.

'We're in!' she said.

'I feel like I've just landed in a spy novel,' Bear said. 'James Bond or something.'

Ruby was furiously clicking on links, working her way through a labyrinth of pages to get to the emissions reports. When she finally found them, she held the sheets Hesse had given her up to the screen and compared the two sets of figures.

'Oh. My. God!' she said.

'How different are they?' Oliver asked.

'Totally different,' Ruby said. 'If these are correct, Hadron has been under-reporting the emissions by at least fifty per cent.'

'Lying, you mean?' Imogen said.

Ruby nodded. 'That would explain the high numbers of lung infections and respiratory disease we've been treating at the clinic. It's been going on for years. Supposedly just coincidence.'

'I hate to be a wet blanket,' Oliver said, finding his lawyer's voice again. 'But we can't be sure these numbers are real. We have to consider the possibility we're being set up.'

'Are you sure you've got no idea who could have left them, Hesse?' Ruby asked.

'None,' he said. 'But why me, anyway? Why wouldn't they give them to you or Oliver?'

'Unless it's someone who knows you,' Oliver said.

It didn't make sense, but Hesse couldn't help thinking of Felicity.

'Anyway, Oliver's right,' Ruby said. 'We can't use them at the meeting. This is our first big public event and Hadron could be setting us up. They'll be ready to pounce on any mistake we make. And this could be a big mistake.'

'What if,' Imogen began, trying to think through the problem the envelope had created. 'What if we said we've got information we can't make public yet, information that has serious consequences for the health of the community. Keep it vague, nothing Hadron could sue over, but enough to set people thinking about their kids and families, about how many of them have been sick. And if it came from a doctor, it would have even more impact.'

Everyone looked at Ruby.

'That could work,' she said.

'We can keep digging after the meeting,' Imogen said. She lined the sheets up on the table and photographed them with her phone. Ruby and Oliver did the same. Then Oliver slipped the originals into his briefcase.

'We need to get moving,' Bear said.

Hesse had been quiet, trying to think through the possibility of Felicity being the source of the figures, but when he snapped back to the present his stomach began to churn again. He hadn't eaten anything, and his breakfast was decorating the garden along the side of the hall. He put two pieces of bread into the toaster. His speech was folded in his back pocket and he touched it for the thousandth time, just to reassure himself. He slathered the toast with butter and ate it quickly, hoping he could keep it down.

The worst of the rain had passed but the sky was still heavy and bruised. Low cloud scudded in from the west and the wind felt like it had ice in it. By the time Hesse got to the hall, the car park was three-quarters full, and it was still thirty minutes before the scheduled start time. He walked up the steps, feeling like a condemned man climbing the scaffold to his execution.

Inside, most of the chairs were filled. The heaters were on and the high windows along each side were fogged. People sat talking in groups, jackets, scarves and coats hanging from the backs of chairs. He knew some from around town—the footy club, the lifesaving club, a few of the older employees at the supermarket. Steve Daly and a couple of other surfers he recognised stood at the side.

People continued to stream through the front door. When all the seats were taken, people spilled into the aisles and across the back wall. There was an overwhelming smell of wet clothes and coffee. A coffee van had set up in the car park and it must have been making a killing. By the time the meeting was ready to start, the hall was packed.

From his seat at the front Hesse scanned the crowd looking for friendly faces. He saw Mus sitting with his family, and Felicity and her father were among a group of men and women wearing Hadron shirts. Felicity held eye contact with him long enough to make him uncomfortable. Then, strangely, she nodded like she was encouraging him.

In the middle of the hall, he spied Rachel Cheng from school. Tina gave him the finger from where she sat, but it was accompanied by something that might have almost been a smile. Skegs was near the front and winked at him. In among the nest of Hadron workers Hesse recognised Stanton, the guy who had photographed him up on the fence a couple of weeks ago, and, beside him, Jago. Jago didn't work for Hadron but he was wearing one of their caps. At the back of the hall, a dozen men in hi-vis shirts with CMU on the front, stood with their hands in their pockets. Hesse guessed they were from the Coal Miners' Union and they'd been brought in for support.

No one could miss the banner plastered across the wall behind the stage and a lot of people were pointing at it and discussing it with others around them.

Hesse looked for Fenna, but he couldn't see her.

At the designated start time, Imogen stood at the microphone. 'Thanks very much for coming everyone. My name is Imogen Stapleton,' she said loudly, and she waited for the crowd to quieten.

Hesse had wondered how his mum would handle the role of MC but as she began to speak, he understood why the group had chosen her. A lot of people knew her—and they'd known his dad. More importantly, she'd been in Shelbourne long enough to be accepted as a local.

Bear sat at the front table with Ruby, Oliver and Samantha, the speaker from Friends of the Earth.

Once Imogen had everyone's attention, she began with an acknowledgment of country. Hesse watched the crowd carefully, trying to distract himself from the tightening knot in his stomach. He read the mood of the room in the faces. Wherever he looked he saw hostility, or neutrality at best.

'We want to emphasise,' Imogen continued, 'that this is

an open forum. We have four speakers and then we'll have questions.'

'Will someone from Hadron speak?' a man called from the back. It was one of the CMU crew. He wore wraparound sunglasses and had a thick, bushy beard.

'The forum has been organised by Shelbourne Action,' Imogen replied, surprised that a question had been asked so early. 'Hadron may wish to hold an information session at another time.'

'Damn right, we will,' another man called, and was met with a smattering of applause.

'Our first speaker,' Imogen said, pressing on, 'is Oliver Bairstow. Oliver is a barrister and his family have had a connection with Shelbourne for more than fifty years.'

'A weekender,' someone called out.

Oliver stood at the microphone and immediately commanded the room. 'I've been coming to Shelbourne on weekends and holidays since I was a child,' he began. 'Some of you may not want to hear it, but everybody in town has a right to decide its future.'

All eyes were on Oliver, who spoke without notes. He'd forgone the casual look and was dressed in a suit. His arguments were direct but clever. He surprised everyone by praising Hadron for its commitment to Shelbourne, its support of local organisations and the employment it generated. Then, slowly and methodically, he turned the argument, explaining Hadron was now leaving Shelbourne, selling up and moving on, and that this was a perfect time to question whether the town wanted a coalmine in its backyard for another fifty years.

'There is no guarantee,' he said, 'that any future buyer would be a good corporate citizen like Hadron has been.'

Hesse thought if he ever had to appear in court, he wanted Oliver as his lawyer. He used words like building materials, constructing a case that sounded so reasonable, secure and safe. But, of course, the kicker came at the end, the call to shut down the mine and power station once and for all. When Oliver finished, to a small round of applause and the general outbreak of talk, he sat down looking pleased with himself. Hesse guessed Oliver must be used to talking in tense situations, laying the ground rules for a discussion when there were conflicting views in the room. It's what lawyers did.

Ruby was next. She'd only been working at the clinic for twelve months but word travels quickly in a small town. She was the first female GP to have stayed for any length of time and most of the women in Shelbourne knew her. Hesse remembered the planning meeting where she'd talked about losing patients if she took a stand against Hadron. And now, here she was, taking a stand.

She looked nervous in a way Hesse hadn't expected, shifting from one foot to the other as she began. There was a different dynamic in the room from when Oliver had spoken. The CMU brigade was having its own conversation. An older woman in the middle turned and glared at them but they kept talking. Hesse could see what was going on. It was because it was a woman speaking, he was sure. The blokes at the back didn't like it and they wanted to make a show of ignoring her. They could accept a female MC, but they weren't going to be lectured about coalmining by a young woman barely out of university.

Ruby took it in her stride and gained confidence as she went, speaking louder over the rumblings at the back. They eventually quietened and she focused on the health issues caused by the emissions from the smokestack.

'How many of you have unexplained coughs all year round?' she asked. 'How many of you have kids with asthma? Why are incidences of lung infections clustered in the streets closest to the pit?'

A man in a Hadron shirt stood up, interrupting Ruby. 'We meet all the EPA requirements,' he said.

'I'm sorry, but—' Ruby tried to continue.

'Sorry, nothin'! You're making accusations against the company. Where's your proof?' the man said, looking to those around him for support.

'And you are?' Ruby asked.

'Brian Pritchard, shop steward at Hadron Shelbourne,' he said belligerently.

A chorus of 'comrade' rippled across the back of the hall.

'Let her speak,' a woman said loudly.

'What you mean,' Ruby said, nodding her thanks to the woman, then addressing Pritchard, 'is that you self-regulate and report to the EPA.'

'Exactly right,' he said.

'If only it were true that you meet all their requirements,' Ruby said.

'What do you mean by that?' Pritchard said, cocking his

chin. The meeting was tilting on an edge and Hesse hadn't even spoken yet.

'I think you know what I mean!' Ruby shot back at him.

The hall erupted. Voices fought with the sound of chair legs scraping the floor as people turned their seats to talk with those around them.

Ruby stood her ground at the microphone and waited.

Bear climbed to his feet and parked himself next to her, towering over the people in the front row. 'All right,' he said, his voice booming even without the help of the PA. 'Let's keep it civilised.'

Slowly, the crowd quietened. 'You'd better have proof,' Pritchard said, before sitting down.

'Shelbourne Action,' Ruby said, her voice composed, 'will be releasing more information about the level of sulphur dioxide emissions from Hadron in the next couple of weeks. Needless to say, this would be a much healthier place to live and raise our kids without an old and inefficient power station burning low-quality brown coal.'

'Says you on your cushy doctor's wage!' Pritchard called out.

'Yeah, what about our jobs?' It was another man in a Hadron cap. He was tall and stocky and stood at the side with his hands wedged into the pockets of a bomber jacket. 'It's all right for you,' he continued, 'you're not going to lose your job. How am I going to feed my kids? Who aren't sick, by the way. They're fit and healthy and thriving.'

The comrades clapped.

Again, Ruby waited. 'This is not a debate,' she said. 'I'm

quoting data from the World Health Organization. There is no safe level of exposure to sulphur dioxide.'

The man puffed his cheeks and shook his head as if he thought Ruby had no idea what she was talking about.

Undeterred, she finished by encouraging everyone to engage in the conversation about the mine, and when they did, to consider the health of future generations.

'And that leads us to our next speaker,' Ruby said. 'Hesse Templeton is seventeen years old and he's concerned about the future not just of Shelbourne, but of the planet. Please welcome him.'

If Hesse had been queasy before, he felt worse now.

He somehow got to his feet, but his legs didn't seem to be connected to his body. Leaning on the table, he sucked in half a dozen deep breaths. Imogen grabbed him firmly by the arm and asked if he was okay. His eyes darted around the room but all the faces had dissolved into a blur. His mouth was clammy and dry. Bear handed him a glass of water as the crowd became impatient.

'Get on with it,' Jago called.

'Give him a chance,' Theo replied.

Hesse moved towards the microphone, knocking the table with his hip and fumbling for the notes in his back pocket. He looked to where Mus was sitting with his family, seeking reassurance from a friendly face. But Mus's eyes were on the floor.

Hesse made it to the microphone, feeling the heat that had built in the hall.

The notes swam in front of his eyes.

Frantically, he scanned the crowd. A trickle of sweat ran down the side of his face. He found Theo, who gave a reassuring nod. And finally, there by the side door, the face he most needed to see—Fenna. She must have arrived late. She was standing with her back against the wall, but once she had his attention, she pushed away from it and stared at him. Her eyes were fierce, and she had her arms crossed, her fists clenched tight.

You've got this, she mouthed.

'G'day,' Hesse began, as much to test the microphone as begin his speech.

The crowd settled and waited.

His notes became clearer but his voice still waivered. 'My name's Hesse, and I'm part of the generation that's going to have to'—he stopped to clear his throat and swallow hard—'to live with the effects of climate change. When most of you are dead, we're the ones who'll have to live in the world you leave behind.'

He paused, expecting a reaction, but there was just silence.

'Climate change will have a huge impact on towns like ours,' he continued, his voice strengthening. 'Unless we stop burning fossil fuels, we are on track for a sea-level rise of at least one metre by 2050. The king tides will flood all the houses along Riverbank Road. Most of the places out at Wangim Point are built on reclaimed swampland. They'll be under water if we can't limit global temperature rise to less than two degrees.'

He and Fenna had given a lot of thought to the speech and had figured it best to hit them where it hurts. 'In fact, half the houses in town are less than a metre above sea level. Unlike the Netherlands'—he shot a glance at Fenna, who smiled—'we haven't built dykes to hold back the sea. Climate change is a fact and burning coal is a major contributor.'

'Rubbish!' someone yelled.

All eyes turned to the middle-aged man who'd leapt to his feet. Hesse didn't recognise him as a local. He was ruddy faced and jowly, dressed conservatively in a suit and tie. In his hand were rolled up notes of his own.

'Sorry, sir,' Bear said, standing up again. 'But Hesse has the microphone. There'll be time for questions soon.'

'I don't have a question,' the man replied. 'I've got a statement. And I'm not going to sit here and be lectured to by a child!'

'Yeah, is he the best you can come up with?' Jago called.

The hall erupted again. People turned one way then the other.

Hesse looked to Imogen, his eyes questioning.

She held her hand up. *Wait*, she mouthed.

He looked around the audience again, searching for support. But his eyes only found the sneering face of Jago.

The conversations fell away when Bear stepped into the centre aisle. 'That's enough,' he boomed.

But the ruddy-faced man stayed on his feet and demanded attention. He squeezed the notes in one hand and gripped the back of the seat in front of him with the other. 'Climate change is a hoax,' he shouted. Spit flew from his mouth and landed in the hair of a woman in front of him.

'Say it, don't spray it,' Tina called out.

This made Hesse smile.

Bear was distracted momentarily and the man took the opportunity to continue. 'These are important issues,' he said. 'Too important for us to be wasting time listening to this boy spouting words someone else has written for him.'

People at the back cheered, but most of the audience waited to see where this would go.

'I—' Hesse started to say.

'Oh, be quiet and sit down,' the man interrupted. 'You're too young to understand. We don't want to hear what you've got to say. Do we?' he asked, looking around the hall for support. 'Do we?' he repeated.

It seemed to Hesse that time slowed then. The humidity in the room somehow added to the weight pushing down on his shoulders. A gust of wind rattled the windows. He was sure everyone had shifted to the edge of their seats, waiting.

A woman sitting near the front passed the toddler she'd been holding to the girl next to her. Then she stood up and faced the man. 'I do!' she said. 'I'm with Hesse.'

'I do too,' yelled Mus, shooting to his feet like he'd just sat on a pin.

'Me too,' called Theo. 'I'm with Hesse.'

'And me,' Steve Daly said loudly.

The call rippled around the room as, one after another, people stood up, some facing the interjector, others making a point of eyeballing the bully boys at the back. Eventually, most of the crowd was standing.

Never one to miss an opportunity, Tina started a chant. 'Hesse! Hesse! Hesse!'

155

It caught on, as people clapped in time and stamped their feet.

Hesse looked to Fenna. She was standing on a table near the exit, her phone in hand, filming. She swung around and gave him the thumbs up. He'd never seen her do that before but in the midst of the chaos, it seemed exactly the right gesture.

Ruby and Oliver stood next to Hesse on one side, Bear and Imogen on the other, as they waited to see what would happen. The Hadron workers were in feverish discussion among themselves, with lots of head-shaking and pointing. Eventually reaching some kind of consensus, they edged their way to the aisle and left the hall, led by Terry Holden. Felicity seemed reluctant to leave but tagged along with her father. The man who'd interjected followed close behind, muttering to himself. The CMU crew were less inclined to give up their position, fanning out across the back wall to emphasise their status in the meeting. But once the chanting and cheering died down, all the attention was back on Hesse.

The rest of his speech was a blur, but he wasn't interrupted again, even though the unionists could be heard exchanging comments at the back. The plan had been to have Samantha speak after him, but Oliver wanted to seize on the momentum Hesse had created. Imogen took the microphone again, thanked everybody for their attendance and encouraged them to come to the front if they had questions.

The meeting ended with an enthusiastic round of applause. It seemed to Hesse that the whole room was buzzing with excitement, though it may just have been the adrenaline still charging through his system.

People he barely knew shook his hand and patted his back. He hardly heard what they were saying. He was too focused on finding Fenna.

When he looked to the back of the hall, the unionists were still standing in a tight group. Jago, who'd stayed when the other Hadron workers had left, was with them and he stared directly at Hesse. He made the shape of a gun with his right hand then lifted his index finger to his mouth, as if blowing away smoke.

Hesse felt a tug on his arm. Fenna pulled him from the middle of the group. 'You were awesome!' she said, kissing him on the cheek. 'And check this out.' She held her phone up and showed him the footage. It looked different from her angle. She'd had the advantage of height, making the crowd seem even bigger, every frame filled with bobbing, talking and shouting heads. And the chorus of '*Hesse, Hesse, Hesse.*'

'We've gotta post this,' she said.

'What do you mean? Why?' Hesse asked.

'Look at it,' she said. 'This is bigger than Shelbourne.'

'She's right.' Rachel Cheng had appeared at his shoulder. Her voice was calm, but her eyes were alive. 'Play it again,' she said.

The three of them hunched over the phone, listening carefully to assess the sound quality.

'I can clean that up,' Rachel said.

'Maybe we should check with Ruby and Oliver before we do anything,' Hesse said.

'It's your footage,' Rachel said to Fenna. 'What do you want to do with it?'

Fenna looked at Hesse and raised an eyebrow, questioning.

Oliver and Ruby were busy talking with the little groups that encircled each of them, while Imogen and Bear were taking down the contact details of a long line of people who wanted to join the campaign.

'She's right,' Hesse said, finally. 'It's your footage.'

'Was anyone else filming?' Rachel asked.

'I couldn't tell,' Hesse said. 'I was too busy shitting myself.'

They laughed then checked the video again, looking for any phones held aloft. Nothing.

'So, you're from the Netherlands, right?' Rachel asked.

Hesse realised she and Fenna hardly knew each other.

'*Ja.*'

'Who do you know there that could help this go big?' Rachel asked.

Fenna smiled. 'Heaps of people.'

13

Hesse and Fenna walked home together. They could hear the noise before they got to the gate. There was a party going on. They entered via the back door and found the kitchen packed. Bear was pumping out toasted cheese sandwiches from the griller, Imogen was making her way through the crowd topping up people's glasses. The concertina doors were pulled back and Ruby and Oliver were holding court in the lounge room.

To Hesse's surprise and embarrassment, everyone stopped and cheered when they saw him and Fenna. Not knowing what else to do, he gave a little wave. Then he shoved his hand back into his pocket.

Oliver stood up on a chair. 'While we've got your attention,' he said, waiting for everyone to quieten down. They all turned to face him. 'Congratulations to everyone who helped get the forum up and running. The letter-writers, the banner-makers, the social-media committee, everyone!'

There was a round of applause.

'And a big shout out to Hesse,' Oliver continued, 'for a great speech. He singlehandedly turned the meeting in our favour.'

Hesse was embarrassed all over again. Fenna had retreated to a corner, but Imogen was beside him and she put her arm around his shoulder to pull him close.

Bear lifted toasties from the griller and slid them onto a plate. 'Here you go, Hesse,' he said. 'Wrap your laughing gear around those.'

As the hubbub of conversation filled the house again, Hesse and Fenna headed for his room, Hesse balancing their toasties on the plate in front of him. It seemed everyone wanted to talk to him. Bob Young waved to him from the hallway and he was just about to make his way over to him when it happened.

First, the discordant sound of shouting outside, then a sudden explosion of glass across the room as the front window shattered. Instinctively, everyone turned away to shield their faces. Hesse dropped the plate when Fenna grabbed him by the arm. There was more angry shouting from the front yard, followed by the revving of an engine and the squeal of tyres as a car took off down the street.

The room was shocked into silence. A brick lay on the floor, and the rug was littered with broken glass. Ruby was the first to move, checking on two older women who had been sitting on the couch by the window. Bear ran up the passageway and out the front door. People who just a minute ago were laughing and celebrating now looked at each other in disbelief, checking to see whether anyone else was injured. Fenna's fingernails dug into Hesse's arm.

The women on the couch were lucky: the largest of the glass shards had caught in the curtains, but they still had small cuts on their arms and hands where they'd covered their heads. Imogen brought the first-aid kit from the bathroom and Ruby moved the women to the chairs in the kitchen.

Bob Young went to pick up the brick, but Oliver held him back.

'Leave it for the police, Bob,' he said. 'There could be prints on it.'

'Are you okay?' Hesse asked Fenna.

'*Nee*,' she stammered. 'I can't believe what just happened.'

'Honestly, this shit never happens here.'

Bear came back inside. 'Don't worry,' he said to Imogen, 'We'll get this cleaned up and I'll ring the glazier.'

Oliver stood in the middle of the lounge room. 'Listen up, everyone,' he said. 'I'm sorry this has happened, Imogen. I'm sure we'll all pitch in to cover the cost.' There was a general nodding of heads. 'We've stirred things up today,' he continued. 'Made some enemies. Not that we didn't know we had them already, but this changes things. We need to be more careful, look out for each other. Did you get a look at the car, Bear?'

'It was just turning the corner at the bottom of the hill,' Bear said. 'Too far away. It might have been a ute, but I can't say for certain.'

'Well, that narrows it down to half the town,' Ruby said.

'What colour?' Hesse asked.

'Not sure. Dark.'

Fenna tightened her grip on Hesse's wrist. Jago drove a black ute.

The party was over. Everyone helped pick up the glass and Vlad Petkovic, the glazier, boarded the window. By the time the police arrived it was just Imogen, Bear, Hesse and Fenna sitting in the kitchen, drinking cups of tea.

Sergeant Howard was the local policeman. He'd been stationed at Shelbourne since the last ice age. He asked all the necessary questions but seemed more interested in getting the details of who was in the house than tracking down the perpetrator. Bear volunteered the information about the ute, but Howard barely bothered to write it down.

'No one was injured, then?' Howard asked.

'Two of our volunteers were badly cut,' Imogen said, barely disguising her anger.

'And where are they now?' the copper asked, looking around the room like they might be hiding somewhere.

'They were treated by a doctor and went home,' Imogen said.

'Not serious then? The injuries, I mean.'

'Nah, nothing serious,' Bear said, his voice hard. 'Just showered by glass after some fuckwit threw a brick through the window.'

Howard stopped writing and stared blankly at Bear. 'Right then,' he said. 'No serious injuries.'

'I gotta say, Sergeant,' Bear said, getting to his feet. 'You don't seem particularly concerned about what's happened here.'

Howard looked up at Bear. 'Off the record,' he began, carefully placing his notebook inside his top pocket, 'what do you expect? You're trying to shut down the biggest employer in town. There's bound to be pushback.'

'Well, off the record, Sergeant,' Bear replied, straightening himself to tower over the copper, 'I expect you to do your job.'

This was a side of Bear Hesse hadn't seen before.

Howard held Bear's gaze long enough to make a point, before his eyes wandered around the kitchen like he was seeing it for the first time. He took in the prayer flags outside the window, the Che Guevara poster on the wall and Imogen's herbal teas lined up in their glass jars on the dresser. He sniffed.

'Right, then. I think I've got all the information I need,' he said.

'Are you going to take the brick?' Imogen asked.

Howard bent and picked it up. 'Sure,' he said, turning it over in his hands. 'Who knows? The owner might come to the station to claim it.' He smirked, pleased with his little joke. 'I'll be in touch,' he said over his shoulder and walked out the front door.

'Prick!' Imogen said.

'He'd be in Hadron's pocket,' Bear said. 'He'd have to be. He's been here too long.'

They sat and talked for another hour, discussing the events of the day until exhausted by them. Fenna had stayed quiet through Howard's visit and Hesse wondered what must have been going through her mind. She'd only been in Shelbourne a couple of weeks, and she'd landed in the middle of the biggest upset the town had seen in his memory.

She nudged Hesse. 'I should go,' she said.

'I'll come with you,' he replied.

'I'd like that.'

'I could drive you,' Imogen said. 'We need to be careful. The brick was a warning.'

Hesse had taken a while to process everything and now he felt more anger than fear. 'We'll be fine, Mum. We can't stop living our lives because one idiot throws a brick through our window.'

'Well, stick together then,' Imogen said.

'Don't reckon that's going to be a problem, actually,' Bear said.

Hesse blushed a little and turned away. Fenna looked at the tabletop like there might be a small diamond lurking among the crumbs.

Hesse grabbed his puffer jacket.

'Here,' Imogen said, handing her jacket to Fenna.

'I'll bring it back tomorrow,' Fenna said.

'No rush,' Imogen said. 'I've got another one.'

It was dark and the street was deserted as they turned down the hill. Leaf scraps and bark rode on the icy wind. They walked towards the river in silence.

Just as they reached the bridge, Hesse's phone buzzed. A message from Rachel: *What do you think?* He and Fenna leaned together and watched the video. Rachel had adjusted the sound, making it clearer. She'd edited the length to a couple of minutes, mercifully cutting out Hesse's fumbling when he first went to the microphone. It captured the intensity in the hall, the chant going up and filling the room. Best of all Fenna had focused on the woman who stood up in the front row, before the commotion began, the first one to say, 'I'm with Hesse.'

Awesome, Hesse texted back. *Now what?*

Rachel's answer was short and to the point. *#I'mWithHesse*

Who do we send it to? Hesse asked.

Everyone.

Hesse and Fenna looked at each other. 'Forward it to me,' Fenna said. 'I'll post it and tag people back home.'

He shook his head. 'I guess I should do the same. But I don't think anyone outside of Shelbourne is going to be interested.'

'We'll see,' she said.

They crossed the bridge and avoided the pub by taking the track along the river, parallel to Riverbank Road. This time Hesse took Fenna's hand, and she leaned into him as they walked.

The path was screened from the road by thin scrub and a stand of moonah. A few minutes on, they heard the low rumble of an engine overtake the crunching of gravel under their feet. There were no car lights visible through the trees, just the sound of the motor. It didn't take them long to realise they were being followed.

When a powerful beam burst through the trees they instinctively dropped to the ground. Hesse guessed it was a shooter's spotlight mounted on the car. It swept across the area. The beam ricocheted off every surface and lit up the river. They held their breath and stayed low. There was no sound other than the growling of the engine, no voices that might give them a clue to who was in the car. The beam slowed and edged closer. Hesse pointed and they crawled towards the protection of a fallen tree a few metres away. Once behind it, they could sit up.

'We need to get out of here,' Hesse whispered.

'No,' Fenna said, her mouth close to his ear. 'I can't move.' Her voice wavered and her breathing was fast, almost panting.

Hesse's heart was racing at a million miles an hour, but the sight of Fenna having a panic attack just made him angry.

The spotlight swung and caught Hesse as he stood up. He shaded his face with his arm, expecting to be hit by something at any second.

'There you are.' It was a man's voice, deep and menacing. Not a voice he recognised immediately but there was something about it that snagged in his memory. It was muffled, like he was talking through a mask or a scarf. 'Got you in the crosshairs now, greenie boy. Bet you thought you were a bit of a hero after that meeting. Not so clever now though, huh?'

To Hesse's surprise, Fenna stood up next to him. They found each other's hand and held on tight. She seemed to vibrate against him.

'Ah, and the girlfriend, too,' the man said. Hesse couldn't be sure, but it sounded as though he was getting closer. There must be two of them, he thought—one on the light, one doing the talking. He moved a little to the right, Fenna shuffling with him. The light followed.

'Like a deer in the headlights!' Another muffled voice, this time from the car.

A stick cracked maybe ten metres away, directly in line with the beam. Hesse tried desperately to think of something to get them away, but nothing came. They were trapped.

The man laughed. Hesse could see him now, a broad silhouette against the light. He was holding something in his hands, a stick. Or a rifle.

'Take this as warning, kid. You need to shut up. Go back to school. Hadron's here to stay,' he said.

The voice was tripping around inside Hesse's brain. Something about it. What was it? *Here to stay.* Who'd said that? Stanton!

Hesse stood a little taller. He tried to control the nervousness in his voice. 'You should stick to chasing kids away from the fence, Stanton. That's what they pay you the big bucks for, isn't it? Must be a lot of responsibility.'

Silence.

Hesse took his chance. 'I wonder what Hadron would think about you hassling a couple of kids. Not a good look for the company, I wouldn't reckon. I might have a chat with Terry Holden.'

'Just out for a bit of spotlighting on a Sunday evening,' Stanton said with a forced laugh. 'No harm in that.'

'Spotlighting? In town? On the river? What're you hoping to shoot?'

'Smartarse,' Stanton said. He whistled loudly and the light shut off. The sound of the shot came almost simultaneously. It was so close Hesse could hear the metallic sound of the rifle as it discharged. He and Fenna fell to their knees again and he felt the gravel dig into the skin through his jeans. Stanton laughed as he crashed through the scrub back to the car. A door slammed, the motor revved, and the car took off in a spray of loose gravel.

Hesse fumbled for his phone and turned on the torch. Fenna had let go of him and was sitting with her arms wrapped around her legs. He squatted next to her. Her breathing was fast and shallow, like she was trying to gulp the air.

'This place,' she wheezed. 'Everything is wrong.' She pulled on a low branch to get to her feet. 'I need to go home,' she said, her voice flat now, exhausted.

Hesse put his arm around her waist as they started walking, but she shrugged it off. At the bottom of the hill leading to the Turners' place she leaned into the slope and strode away from him. 'Thanks,' she said over her shoulder.

'See you tomorrow?' Hesse called after her.

She didn't reply. Didn't turn around. Hesse watched as her shape faded between streetlights, then re-emerged under the next one's glow. At the top of the hill, she opened the gate and disappeared.

He was careful on his way home, keeping to the well-lit streets. Just as he crossed the bridge, his phone pinged. It was Rachel: *It's happening*! There was a link to her Twitter feed. The video already had a hundred and fifty likes and thirty retweets.

Hesse had hardly ever used Twitter. He and Fenna had only joined to keep Oliver happy. He'd never even sent a tweet, so he was unsure whether a hundred and fifty likes were good or not. It seemed like a lot.

He retweeted the video and tagged Fenna.

14

Hesse tried to ignore the buzzing of his phone. He had it on silent but it vibrated incessantly. He had no idea of the time but it was barely light. It was Monday—and a public holiday. Theo was opening late so he didn't need to be at work until nine-thirty. He threw the phone at the stack of dirty clothes on the floor then buried his head in the pillow and wrapped it around his ears. Still, he could hear it.

'Shit. Shit. Shit!' he mumbled as he crawled to the end of the bed and reached for the phone. The home screen was lit up like a Christmas tree with alerts on Twitter, WhatsApp, Instagram and Messages. He had five missed calls.

He opened Messages first. There were ten: seven from Rachel and others from Mus and Tina. He looked at Rachel's: *Check*

Twitter! The second one was more expressive: *Holy shit!* He quickly flicked through the others, all variations on the same theme. Rachel's last message said: *#I'mWithHesse is trending!* He didn't exactly know what that meant but he figured it must be good.

When he opened Twitter, his mouth fell open. The video had seventy thousand likes and twenty-five thousand retweets. The numbers kept increasing as he watched, ticking over like someone was cranking a wheel at the side. He flicked back to his Twitter profile. He hadn't bothered to load a pic or a background shot, but overnight he'd somehow gathered nearly ten thousand followers. Ten thousand! He scrolled through them. There were a few he recognised from the campaign but most of them he didn't—and they were from all over the world. A lot from Europe.

He hadn't even got to Instagram or WhatsApp when Rachel called. He desperately wanted to talk to Fenna, but he picked up.

'Can you believe this?' she said.

'What? How?' He was lost for words.

'Incredible, isn't it? I'm guessing Fenna's responsible for most of it.'

'What do you mean?'

'She was going to post to friends in Europe, right?'

'Yeah, she said she would.'

'Any idea who they were?'

'Nope. But I'm about to call her.'

'This is big, Hesse. Huge. You'd better prepare yourself.'

He waited for her to explain.

'Look through the comments,' she said. 'And don't take anything personally. We've made a splash and the trolls are out in force.'

'Why would trolls come after me?'

'Hesse, you need a crash course in the twenty-first century. You're in the eye of a shitstorm. Is there someone down there you can get to help you?' Rachel lived in Castlereagh.

'Mum's here, but she'd be as useless as I am with Twitter.'

'It won't just be Twitter. The media will feed on this like sharks. They watch for trends and jump on anything that looks like a good story.'

'How do you know all this?'

'You know the Climate Strike we've been advertising at school? We've been using Twitter for ages. You won't believe what one post can do.'

'I just picked up ten thousand followers overnight. I think I believe.'

'Oliver Bairstow, the dude that spoke at the meeting yesterday, I followed him last night and checked his posts. He's pretty savvy for an old guy. Can you get him to help you?'

'I guess so, if he hasn't gone back to Melbourne.'

'Get onto him, Hesse. Now,' she said, and hung up.

Before he checked anything else he called Fenna. It rang through to message bank.

He instantly tried again.

When she answered her voice was husky and dry. *'Ja.'*

'Hey, it's me. How are you doing?'

'I'm so tired.' Her voice trailed off.

'You haven't heard?'

'Heard what?'

'The video. The hashtag. They've gone ballistic. It's got thousands of hits. Tens of thousands.'

'What? Really?' She sounded more alert. 'Hesse, that's so great.'

'Who did you send it to last night?'

'Just some friends at home.'

'Who exactly?'

She thought for a minute. 'Anne, Marieke, Kees, Katie, Wim—'

'Who are they? What do they do?'

'I told you I know people! Have you heard of Generation Climate Europe? Look them up. And Anne's parents work for the UN, in climate policy. You've heard of the UN, right?'

He laughed. 'Yeah, I've heard of the UN.'

'Oh, and Kees' sister works for the European Climate Foundation.'

'But we're just a little town at the arse end of the world. Why would they be interested in us?'

'That's not what the brochures said when I applied for the exchange.'

He liked her dry humour. 'You didn't answer my question,' he said.

'It's the video. It's powerful stuff, Hesse.'

'And you made it!'

'*Ja*. By accident. Rachel did the hard work.'

Imogen knocked at his door. 'Hesse, are you awake?'

173

'Gotta go,' he said to Fenna. 'Can you come over this morning?'

'Sure,' she said before the line went dead.

Imogen stuck her head in the door. 'My phone's going crazy. What's happened?'

He sat up. 'Come and look at this, Mum. We're famous.'

She pulled up a chair next to the bed and he showed her the video.

'Did you ask Oliver before you posted it?'

'No.'

She took a deep breath and exhaled. 'Well, you probably should have. But it seems pretty harmless. What's the fuss?'

'Look.' He showed her his Twitter feed. 'It's gone all around the world. Viewed'—he checked the current number—'nearly a hundred thousand times.'

'What? Overnight?' She was incredulous. 'How come?'

'We've hit a nerve, Mum.'

'How do they know about our campaign?'

'They probably don't. It's about the video, about kids not being listened to.'

The smell of pancakes wafted into the room. 'Bear's doing breakfast,' she said, standing up.

'Mum,' Hesse grabbed her arm. 'Rachel reckons we might get calls from TV and radio today.'

'Let's not get ahead of ourselves, Hesse. Come and have some breakfast.'

Bear was sitting at the table, a stack of pancakes on a plate in front of him. 'You're up early,' he said as Hesse sat down.

'Think it's going to be a busy day.'

'Hungry?'

'Starving,' he replied.

Imogen poured coffee for herself and Bear. Hesse's phone continued to ping. A message came through from Rachel: *Turn on channel 7*

By the time he found the remote and switched it on, the video was almost finished. The chant was reverberating around the hall and people were on their feet clapping in time. The footage was grainier on the big screen. They cut back to a panel of two women and a man. The women were mirror images of each other, tall, thin, blonde, orange-tinted skin. The man was older, balding but with the teeth of someone much younger.

'The video, apparently taken at a meeting in Shelbourne yesterday, has gone viral,' the man said. 'I'm interested in your thoughts, Tanya. You know the town well, don't you?'

'Yes I do, Fitzy,' said the woman on his left. 'My family have been holidaying in Shelbourne for three generations. And I have to tell you, it's a disgrace what's happening down there. Hadron has been the lifeblood of that town for fifty years. It is a huge employer and it's been very, very generous in supporting—'

'Yes, but what about this video?' Fitzy interrupted.

'Fitzy, if you'll let me finish! The video shows just how angry the town is with this group trying to block the sale of the mine and power station.'

'Does it?' Fitzy asked. 'They seem to be supporting the young boy speaking. And the hashtag says *I'm With Hesse.*'

'And look,' the other woman said, holding up her phone.

'It's getting massive numbers on Twitter.'

'Chatter on Twitter doesn't mean anything,' Tanya replied, struggling to retain her composure. 'This is just selfish activists trying to put honest people out of work.'

'Anyway,' Fitzy said, 'we're doing our best to track down Hesse and find out what all the fuss is about. And coming up next, the weight-loss pill that will change your life forever.'

Hesse turned the TV off.

'Bloody hell,' Bear said. 'Fitzy's tracking you down. You *are* famous.'

Hesse didn't know what to think. When he went to bed last night, barely anyone outside Shelbourne knew he even existed.

There was a knock at the front door. 'That'll be Fitzy,' Bear said, trying not to laugh. 'Once he's on your case there's no stopping him.'

Imogen opened the door. It was Oliver and Ruby. 'You've heard, then,' Imogen said.

Oliver's face was equal parts concern and excitement, while Ruby was in the middle of a call as they came down the hallway.

'What do you think?' Ruby was saying. She listened for a while longer. 'Okay,' she eventually replied. 'I'll talk to him.' She hung up.

Imogen poured coffee for Oliver and Ruby while Hesse started on the pancakes.

'The video is great,' Oliver began. 'But you should have talked to the group before you put it online.'

Hesse paused with a pancake dripping honey halfway to his mouth. 'It's Fenna's video,' he said defensively. 'She can do what she likes with it.'

Ruby sipped her coffee. 'It's okay, Hesse,' she said. 'We're not blaming you. It's done now, so we just have to go with it.'

'We could have used it more strategically,' Oliver said.

'It's got a hundred thousand likes on Twitter,' Hesse said. 'How much more strategic do you want?'

Phones continued to buzz and ping around the room. Bear was mixing more pancake batter.

'Who was that you were talking to?' Imogen asked Ruby.

'3GD radio. They want to interview Hesse.'

Hesse was onto his third pancake. Everything up to that point had been exciting and surreal. But he didn't like the idea of being interviewed.

'I spoke to Ray Addison's producer, Amber Nguyen,' Ruby said. 'Addison does the morning program. Amber recognised me in the video. I did a studio segment on rural doctors a couple of months ago.'

'Addison can go in pretty hard,' Oliver said. 'I've heard him do some tough interviews. But it's a big opportunity for the campaign. What do you think, Hesse?'

Hesse looked at Imogen and she shrugged. He felt the same churning in his gut that had overtaken him yesterday at the meeting.

There was a tap at the back door and Fenna stepped into the kitchen. Her eyes dropped to the floor as soon as she saw the people crowded around the table. Imogen pulled out a chair and Fenna sat down next to Hesse. He felt for her hand under the table.

'What would I say,' Hesse asked.

'Here,' Oliver said, pushing a piece of paper across the table. 'It's a list of my talking points from the meeting. Don't let him fluster you. Stay calm.'

Everything had happened so quickly since Hesse had been woken by his phone. He realised he hadn't told anyone about the incident with Stanton last night.

'Okay,' he said, finally. 'I'll do it.'

Ruby was already tapping at her phone, afraid he'd change his mind. She asked that the interview be recorded rather than broadcast live. 'Great,' she said when they agreed. 'Five minutes? We'll wait for your call. Just remember he's seventeen.'

Hesse was still getting his head around the talking points when Ruby's phone rang again. She answered and listened for a few seconds. 'Yes, he's here.' She held the phone to her chest. 'You need somewhere quiet,' she said to Hesse.

'I'll do it in my bedroom,' he said.

Imogen stood up as Ruby handed him the phone. 'No, I'm fine, Mum. I'll do it on my own.' He took the phone and walked to his room.

The interview was a blur. They did most of it in one take, telling him they'd edit it before it went to air. When it finished, he sat and stared at the wall, hoping it would play well. There was a lot riding on it.

The kitchen was busier still. More people had arrived. Vlad Petkovic was fitting new glass in the lounge-room window and Oliver was on the phone talking to a reporter. Ruby's phone buzzed and Hesse passed it to her before she could ask how the interview went. There were more pancakes and toast and tea. The radio was on and Hesse recognised Addison's voice. It wasn't his interview though. He was talking about a couple of bushwalkers lost near Mount Hotham. Theo had appeared out of nowhere and stood by the sink with a coffee in his hand. He raised his cup to Hesse. 'You'll be busy today,' he said. 'I'll handle the shop.'

Hesse looked for Fenna. 'Out the back,' Imogen said.

He found her sitting on the seat by the shed. She was wearing Imogen's puffer jacket. She had her knees tucked up and was scrolling her phone. 'How did it go?' she asked.

'Honestly,' he said, 'it might be okay or it might be complete shit.'

She smiled. 'Come. Sit,' she said, patting the bench beside her.

'How did I end up here, Fenna? Talking on the radio like I'm some sort of authority on this stuff.'

'I don't know, but you've got lots of fans. The video's up to two hundred and fifty thousand likes. And a hundred thousand retweets.'

'So, I'm becoming a bigger target by the minute.'

'Promise you'll still like me when you're rich and famous?'

This made him laugh.

'Okay, just famous then,' she said.

'Famous enough to be exposed as a fraud with three weeks research on a school project behind me.'

'People hear this stuff from experts all the time. Maybe they just want to hear it from someone like them.'

Oliver stuck his head out the door. 'Hesse,' he called, 'the interview's on after the news. Five minutes.'

'Come on,' Fenna said. 'Time to face the music.'

15

The air of expectation in the kitchen made Hesse even more nervous. The whole house smelled of food. Imogen sidled up to him and looped her arm through his. Fenna did the same on the other side.

The news finished with the weather report: scattered showers, light and variable winds to fifteen knots on the bay and a top temperature of eighteen degrees. Hesse noted the variable winds. It might be offshore this morning.

Then Addison began. '*The small coastal town of Shelbourne is on edge this morning after a controversial town meeting turned violent yesterday. The forum finished in uproar and led to a brick being thrown through the window of a member of Shelbourne Action, the environment group that called the* meeting. Sources in the town say the community is split over the sale or potential closure of the Hadron coalmine and power station. Closure would put eighty people out of work and decimate the town's economy. A video of the near-riot in the Shelbourne Community Hall has gone viral and, incredibly, has spread around the world overnight. I've got one of the speakers from the meeting on the line this morning. Hesse Templeton is a high-school student and spokesperson for Shelbourne Action. Good morning, Hesse.'

'G'day.'

Hesse cringed at how nervous he sounded.

'You were at the centre of the action yesterday. What happened?'

'Well, the meeting was actually pretty chill until—'

'Chill? That's not what I saw on the video. It looked like a riot.'

'It wasn't a riot. There were two speakers before me and no interruptions. Everyone was listening.'

'But things turned nasty, didn't they?'

'A couple of people wanted to interrupt but—'

'You were shouted down, weren't you?'

'They didn't like what I was saying.'

'And what were you saying, Hesse?'

'Just the facts. You know, that climate change is real and we need to move to renewables.'

'And you're an expert on this, are you? How old are you, mate?'

'I'm seventeen and, no, I'm not an expert but I live in

Shelbourne, and we know Hadron is selling up and leaving so it's a good chance to shut down the power station. It's old and dirty and—'

'And you'll be putting eighty people out of work.'

'No, *we won't be. Hadron will. The workers are its responsibility.'*

Oliver gave Hesse a thumbs up.

Addison laughed then. '*Sorry, son*'—Hesse wondered what happened to *mate*—'*but you sound a bit too young to understand what you're talking about. I'm surprised the group put you in front of a microphone.'*

'Well, you'll be surprised that a quarter of a million people have liked the video on Twitter.'

'Hits on Twitter don't put food on the tables of families when people lose their jobs.'

Hesse hadn't known how to respond. Addison's producer had cut in and asked if he was still on the line and if he wanted to continue. He had scrambled to look over Oliver's notes, trying to find an answer. Now, they'd edited out the break.

'We just think Hadron has had a fair go in Shelbourne. It's been here for fifty years. We appreciate what it's done for the town but there's no place for a coalmine and a dirty old clunker of a power station on our beautiful coastline.'

'Well, you haven't convinced me, Hesse, but I appreciate you taking our call.'

He was cut off before he had the chance to reply.

The kitchen burst into applause. Even Vlad Petkovic had stopped his work on the window to listen.

Oliver shushed everyone and pointed back to the radio. Addison was welcoming another guest, Adrian Nutt.

'This should be interesting,' Oliver said. Most people seemed to know who Nutt was, but Hesse had no idea. 'He's got his own TV show,' Oliver quickly explained. 'His nickname is Nutt Job.' He put his phone on top of the fridge next to the radio to record the interview.

Nutt sounded angry from the start and Addison egged him on rather than interrupting him like he had Hesse. It was more of a rant than an interview.

'*I have to say, Ray, I'm utterly disgusted at what happened in Shelbourne yesterday. This is the sort of thing fair-minded Australians hate—uninformed, angry alarmists spouting their climate-change propaganda. And do you know what the worst of it was?*' He didn't wait for Addison to respond. '*They put a child up in front of the microphone to peddle their lies.*'

Everyone in the kitchen turned to look at Hesse. He stuck his thumb in his mouth and sucked it. They laughed.

But Nutt wasn't finished. '*People like this need to understand that coal is Australia's future. They carry on about renewables but everyone knows they are unreliable. I mean, what happens when the wind stops blowing and, I hate to break it to*'—there was a pause while he obviously checked his notes—'*to Shelbourne Action, but the sun doesn't shine at night!*'

'There are batteries that can store solar, Adrian,' Addison said.

Nutt ignored him. '*Australia only contributes a tiny amount to global emissions but idiots like the ones getting all the* attention in Shelbourne want to destroy people's livelihoods so they can feel good about themselves. And mark my words, Ray, it's all about them getting attention. It's got nothing to do with the great hoax of global warming.'

When Nutt finished, Oliver reached up and switched off the radio. 'Thank you, Mister Nutt,' he said.

'What do you mean,' Bear asked. 'He laid into us. Called us idiots.'

'Exactly,' Oliver replied. 'And that's good for us.'

'How?' Imogen asked.

'He's no different to the guy who interrupted Hesse at the meeting yesterday. And look how the crowd turned on him. All we have to do is post a couple of Nutt's quotes about climate change being a hoax and coal being Australia's future. People like Nutt don't understand media has moved on. By the time Addison's finished his show this morning, we'll have spread those quotes all over the world.'

'That's great,' Bear said, 'but how are people overseas going to help close a power station in Shelbourne.'

Hesse thought Oliver would make a good teacher. He was patient with everyone. 'Hadron is a multinational company, trying to rebrand as a clean, green power generator. So, the more attention we can draw to its dirty little secret in Shelbourne, the more uncomfortable its shareholders are going to be.'

'And the less likely it will be to find a company to buy into Shelbourne,' Ruby added.

'Meaning Hadron could be left with no option other than to shut it down,' Oliver concluded.

Hesse thought Oliver and Ruby were ten steps ahead of everyone else in the room.

'So, what do we do now?' Imogen asked.

'Let our fingers do the talking,' Ruby said. 'And make sure we tag Hadron in every tweet. We need the company, and their shareholders, to see the interest we're generating.'

It was only nine-thirty but Hesse was exhausted. So much had happened in the last couple of days, and now he needed some Hesse-time.

He whispered to Fenna. 'Want to come to the beach?'

'*Ja*,' she said, and they slipped out the back door.

It was still cool but the sky was cloudless and the sun was above the ridge.

'We can get a foamy from Theo,' Hesse said.

'It'll take too long,' Fenna replied. 'I can share yours.'

Hesse stuck his head through the door and told Imogen where they were going. She was hunched over her phone but nodded distractedly. Then he grabbed their wetsuits and towels and loaded an old board of his dad's onto the carrier. They rode out to Corrals. Hesse knew it would be quiet there. It was the last day of the long weekend and a lot of people would be packing up for the drive back to Melbourne.

They changed quickly, turning their backs to each other under the cover of the tea trees. Fenna slid easily into her new wetsuit. As they bundled their clothes and stashed them in the crate on the back of his bike, Hesse noticed the undies and bra in Fenna's pile. 'No *zwimmers* today,' she explained, with the hint of a smile.

The tide was low, exposing a hundred metres of sand leading to the water. There was a small swell running and, while the wind wasn't offshore, it was light enough not to be affecting the waves.

They waded out until it was deep enough for Hesse to climb onto his board. Fenna dived under an approaching wave, rolled onto her back and spread her arms. Her hair fanned out in a dark halo. The sun caught the droplets of water on her face and her eyes shone. She rolled again and swung her arms over in an easy freestyle. Hesse paddled next to her, keeping an eye on the horizon for any sign of a set. Eventually, they stopped and Fenna rested her arms on the board. Hesse slid off the side and they faced each other across the board, their legs dangling below.

'You did so great in the interview,' Fenna said.

'I'd have been lost without Oliver's notes.'

'It didn't sound like it.' She sat her chin on her folded arms.

Looking past her he saw a small set approaching. He pulled the board underneath him as Fenna pushed away to tread water. The peak was a little to his left so he paddled into position and put in half a dozen strong strokes, feeling the familiar surge as the wave lifted under him. He popped to his feet, took the little drop, pulled a fast bottom turn then milked the wall until it closed out on the shore break. The ride lasted no more than ten seconds, but it was a release, something so instinctive he hardly realised he was doing it.

Fenna had swum out beyond the peak. She was fifty metres away when she turned and came back towards him. She moved quickly, her stroke powerful, breathing to both sides, her body gliding through the water.

They swam and surfed for another hour, each wave interspersed with a little conversation about life or school or friends. Fenna took a few tries to get to her feet on the board but eventually rode a wave to the beach. For a while the campaign and all the hassles that went with it seemed a million miles away. The sun gently warmed them and the water held them in its spell.

When they had exhausted themselves, they made their way into the shallows and sat for a while with the waves lapping at their feet. Fenna's eyes stayed fixed on the horizon, but Hesse couldn't stop looking at her. Her face glowed and her hair was swept back in a dark sheen.

She sensed him watching. 'What?' she said, turning to look at him.

He wanted to say she was beautiful. That he had never met anyone like her. But the words couldn't find a way out. A smile would have to do.

'Come on,' he said, getting to his feet and offering her his hand. 'We should get back. They'll be wondering where we are.'

'They'll be wondering where *you* are. No one cares about me, Hesse. Just Aunt Lydia. And she'd rather I was tied up in the basement.'

He laughed. 'I didn't know the Turners had a basement.'

'She's digging one. I hear her at night.'

They held hands as they walked up the path through the dunes. Back at the bikes, Hesse handed a towel to Fenna.

'Help me unzip,' she said, turning around.

Hesse pulled at the tag and watched as her wet skin was

exposed all the way down her back, her vertebrae standing out like buttons below her wide shoulders. She rolled the suit off to her waist and wrapped the towel around herself, leaned over and hopped from one foot to the other to get out of the legs. Then she turned and stood in front of him. He felt rooted to the spot. She took a step forward and kissed him, softly at first but then with her whole body pushed against him. He looped his arms around her, bringing his hands up onto her bare shoulders to smooth away the droplets of water that had fallen from her hair. Her skin was cool and the towel was damp between them.

She playfully pushed him back then, retrieved her clothes from the crate and walked behind a low-standing tea tree. As she dressed, Hesse changed quickly, and they followed the tracks out to the road. They crested the top of the hill by the lookout and coasted down towards town. Fenna was slightly ahead of him as they picked up speed.

She called over her shoulder, 'I think we should have sex.'

Hesse thought he must have misheard. He pedalled up next to her. 'What did you say?' he asked.

'I said, we should have sex.' There was no grin to make him think she was joking. She was looking down the hill, her face perfectly composed.

'Okay,' he said. 'When?'

'Soon.'

She pushed ahead and beat him to the corner at the Fat Controller by a good ten metres. She was up on the pedals, her body arched forward, streamlining. He tried to catch her but the board in the carrier slowed him down. Finally, she stopped before the bridge and waited for him.

'I've got homework to do,' she said. 'Call me later?'

'Okay,' he said, hardly hearing her. All he could think of was what she'd said coming down the hill.

She kissed him, quick and cool, like someone might be watching. Then she rode away and crossed the bridge.

Hesse turned towards home. As he passed the front of the surf shop Theo called to him. 'Oi! I thought you were going to be busy today. Didn't know you'd be out surfing with your girlfriend.'

Hesse pulled onto the footpath and came to a stop on the concrete verge by the second-hand board racks. 'Just needed a quick one,' he said. 'It's been crazy since yesterday.'

'How was it?' Theo asked.

'Small but clean. Just a little bank at Corrals.'

Theo stroked his beard. 'You'd better come in and have a look at this,' he said, walking into the shop.

Hesse leaned his bike against the wall and followed Theo through to the shaping bay. The pungent smell of fresh resin filled the air.

'It'll need to cure for a week or so.'

In the middle of the room, resting on the padded rack, was his new board. Theo must have glassed it last night. It was bright red and it glinted under the lights. Hesse moved around it, bending to look at the thickness of the rail and the upward lift of the rocker.

'It'll be perfect for Razors,' Hesse said.

Theo sat on the stool in the corner and picked up an empty coffee cup off the floor. He turned it over in his hands. Hesse knew Theo's moods and when he went quiet like this, he usually had something to say.

'What's up?' Hesse asked.

Theo sat forward with his elbows on his knees, twirling the empty cup in his hands. 'Razors,' he said. 'You've never asked me about what happened the day your dad died out there.'

'He paddled out on his own and disappeared. There's not much more I need to know.' Hesse had never attempted to bury the memory. It was the first thing the counsellor had told him. He'd tried, as much as a ten-year-old could, to keep the conversation open about losing his father. But there'd come a time when the conversation had exhausted itself and there didn't seem any point returning to it again and again.

'I was supposed to be surfing with him that afternoon, but I was held up. Do you know how often I've regretted being late that day?'

'It's not your fault, Theo. Dad chose to go out on his own.'

'Once he set himself to do something, there was no stopping him,' Theo said, shooting a smile at Hesse. 'Like someone else I know.'

'Is that why you made me the board—because you know I'm going to surf Razors?'

'You don't have to, you know. You won't find any answers out there. Sometimes shit just happens and there's no explanation for it.'

'I know,' Hesse said. 'But maybe it's something I want to

do for me, regardless of what happened to Dad.'

Theo nodded.

Hesse turned towards the door then stopped. 'Why now?' he asked. 'Why bring up Dad now?'

Theo looked up from his chair in the corner. 'Because of the speech,' he said. 'You reminded me of him. He never shirked a challenge—always saw things through.'

When Hesse got home, there were cars parked out the front with TV station logos along their sides. He almost turned around, but Bear was leaving and he spotted him.

'You'd better get in there, mate,' he said. 'Your mum's herded them into the backyard but they all want to speak to the man of the moment.'

Hesse sighed. 'I said everything in the radio interview. What more do they want?'

'They all want to hear the same thing,' Bear replied. 'And they'll still call it an exclusive on tonight's news.' He gave Hesse a pat on the shoulder as he walked out the front gate. 'I've got a shift at the pub. Double time and a half on a public holiday. See you later.'

Hesse pushed his bike up the driveway to the back of the house. Imogen was waiting for him. 'Where have you been?' she asked, looking harried. 'These people have been waiting for ages.'

'I told you I was ducking out for a while.'

'You've been gone for two hours, Hesse.'

'Sorry. Fenna and I, we—'

He didn't get the chance to finish his sentence. The reporters moved towards him, phones in their hands, followed by others lugging cameras. He found himself backed up against the shed, still gripping the handlebars of his bike.

'Okay, okay,' Imogen said to the group. 'Let him get his breath first.' She hustled him into the shed where they could speak privately. 'Are you okay to do this, Hesse?'

Hesse liked this about his mum—the way she moved past anger quickly, letting it go before it caused any damage.

'Yeah, I'm fine,' he said, though the butterflies were rioting in his stomach again.

'Something has happened since your interview this morning,' she said, shaking her head. 'You won't believe it.'

'What?'

'Have you checked your phone?'

'No. You know I never take it to the beach. Just tell me, mum. You're making me even more nervous.'

She smiled and said, 'Greta Thunberg retweeted the video!'

'Holy shit,' he said, as much to himself as his mum. 'Holy, holy shit!'

'It's incredible, I know. And now everyone wants to talk to you. We've been taking calls all morning.' She straightened his T-shirt and brushed the hair off his face.

Hesse was shepherded to the side of the yard with the best light and without the clothesline in shot. The crews spread around him in a half circle. He looked past them to see people spilling out of the house to watch.

Oliver came and stood beside him. 'Just remember, everyone,' he said in his best lawyer's voice, 'Hesse has never done this before, so take it easy. I'll close down the interview if I have to.'

'Yeah sure, mate,' one of the cameramen said, impatiently. 'Can we just get on with it. We're on a deadline here.'

Oliver's stare could have stopped a charging bull in its tracks. He leaned into Hesse and whispered, 'Don't feel you have to respond if you're not comfortable with the question. And keep your answers short.'

Hesse took a deep breath.

'How does it feel to have your video going around the world?' a reporter asked.

He'd anticipated this one. 'It's not my video, a friend filmed it. But it's good that the campaign is getting attention.'

'This is bigger than Shelbourne, though, isn't it?'

He couldn't tell through the glare of the camera lights who was asking the question. 'The meeting yesterday was all about Shelbourne. We want to shut down the mine and stop Hadron polluting the air with emissions from the power station,' he replied.

'Why do you think the video went viral, Hesse?'

'I'm not sure. Maybe because I'm young and people like that.'

'Adrian Nutt doesn't like it. What have you got to say to Mr Nutt?'

'I'd never heard of him until this morning,' Hesse said honestly, raising a few chuckles from the film crews. 'But I don't care what he thinks.'

'He's a powerful voice. Why should people listen to a teenager instead of an experienced journalist like Nutt?'

'Look at Greta Thunberg. She's not much older than me. I

mean, has Adrian Nutt ever spoken at the UN? Is he invited to international climate talks?'

'Are you comparing yourself to Greta Thunberg?'

'Shit no! Sorry. I mean, no, of course not. I'm just a kid from Shelbourne.'

'And what about Greta supporting you? How does that feel?'

'Pretty surreal.'

There were more questions about how old he was and what school he went to but one by one the camera crews packed up. Eventually Hesse and Oliver went back to the house.

Hesse felt all the energy had been drained from his body. He sat down at the kitchen table, stretched and let the tension go from his shoulders.

'Handled like a pro,' Ruby said.

Imogen put a glass of Milo in front of him and he downed it in one go.

There were still people in the lounge room, all tapping away at their phones and laptops.

'It's been crazy here today,' Ruby said. 'It's amazing what one video can do. Have you heard of the Environmental Defender's Office?'

Hesse shook his head.

'They're lawyers who work to help environmental causes. I spoke to them this morning and they've agreed to look at the emissions figures we got yesterday. They'll be able to tell us whether they're genuine or not.'

So much had happened since yesterday, Hesse had almost forgotten about the mysterious envelope.

16

There were more interview requests through the afternoon, but Oliver, Imogen and Ruby dealt with them. Hesse walked down the hallway and closed the bedroom door behind him. He was drained from everything that had happened in the last twenty-four hours: the meeting, the brick through the window, the spotlighting incident, the video going viral, the interviews. All of them were crowding for space in his mind, but one thing overrode them all—Fenna wanted to have sex with him.

He lay back on the bed and pulled his phone out of the drawer. There were thousands of comments under his tweets and the ones he was tagged in. Ignoring Rachel's advice, he scrolled through them. She was right. There were lots of supporters but just as many haters. Those ones liked capitalising their comments: TOO YOUNG TO KNOW WHAT HE'S TALKING ABOUT, STUPID, ARROGANT, JOB WRECKER, PRIVILEGED, SHOULD BE SHOT. That last one brought him to his senses. He quit Twitter and went to Messages. There were more than thirty of them, mostly from kids at school, even a couple from teachers. He wondered how they'd got his number. At least they were all positive, congratulating him and wishing him luck.

There was nothing from Jake.

At the bottom was a number he didn't recognise. *The figures are real. I can prove it. Meet me at the boatshed @8.* Hesse reread the message. It came from someone who didn't know him well enough to be in his contacts, but they'd got hold of his number. And they knew about the boatshed.

Since the meeting, he'd been thinking more about Felicity, the way she'd looked at him and nodded her encouragement. She could have access to information through her dad. But it didn't make sense. She'd argued against Hesse in class and told him the campaign was a waste of time. And even if it was her, she could be setting him up.

The rest of the afternoon passed slowly as Hesse pulled himself back into the real world of homework and school. He'd allowed assignments to stack up while he prepared for the meeting and now he faced a tsunami of overdue essays and exercises. It wasn't so bad once he got started, his phone back in the drawer and his noise-cancelling headphones cutting out the voices from the kitchen.

Imogen knocked on his door a few minutes before the evening

news. She cocked her head towards the lounge room. 'Come on, big shot,' she said, smiling. 'Let's watch it with the others.'

Most of the people had left but Oliver and Ruby were still there. Some of the interviews with Hesse were already up online. The Ray Addison one, and Adrian Nutt's commentary afterwards, were dominating news feeds and #I'mWithHesse was still trending on Twitter.

Imogen flicked between the two main channels. They were the third item on Channel Seven, after a car fire on the M80 and the missing hikers on Mount Hotham. The reporter made a big deal of how the video had gone viral and been supported by Greta Thunberg. Then they cut to an interview with Terry Holden. He brushed off the confrontation at the meeting, saying how great it was that we lived in a country where people could express their opinions. When the reporter questioned him about emissions from the power station, he said the company had an impeccable environmental record.

'We'll see about that,' Ruby said.

Finally, there was Hesse in the backyard, his hair still wet from the surf and his voice sounding so much less confident than Holden's. They only showed two of the questions he'd answered before they cut back to the reporter standing outside the Hadron gates as workers filed out at the change of shift. She looked directly into the camera and said, 'These are the men and women whose livelihoods are at stake in this bitter confrontation that has divided Shelbourne. They stand to lose everything if a buyer can't be found and the mine and power plant are forced to close. Kylie Winter. Seven News. Shelbourne.'

The report on Channel Nine was pretty similar. Their reporter had asked one of the workers leaving the power station what he thought of the situation. There was a close-up of his weathered face, the worry lines across his forehead creased with coal dust.

'Sorry,' he said, ducking away from the camera. 'The company has asked us not to comment.' He hesitated and turned back to face her. 'But I'll say this. Everyone at that meeting yesterday went home and used electricity to charge their laptops and phones and cook their dinners. And where do ya reckon that electricity comes from?'

When the newsreader went to an ad break, Imogen switched the TV off.

'Was that good or bad?' Hesse asked Oliver.

'Both,' Oliver replied. 'It's all in the way they frame the story. They're not interested in being objective. They'll find the human-interest angle and workers losing their jobs in a small town always plays well.'

'So, what was good about it?' Imogen asked.

'We're on the news to start with,' Oliver responded. 'Not everyone's on social media and there may be half a million more people who know about our campaign now. We've got the youth angle with Hesse and the video from the meeting works for us—a teenager being attacked by a climate-change denier.' He smiled. 'Not a bad weekend's work.'

It was a relief when Ruby and Oliver left. Imogen poured herself a glass of wine and sat opposite Hesse at the kitchen table. It felt like they hadn't had the place to themselves for days.

'Hungry?' she asked.

'Starving.'

'Business as usual then.'

'Yep.'

'Soup and toasties, what do you reckon?'

'Sounds good to me.'

Imogen had a way of knowing how he felt without him having to explain. He'd had it up to the eyeballs with the campaign and videos and seeing his face plastered across screens. What he needed as much as food was a bit of normality.

He helped his mum chop the veggies. She'd put on her music, some wafty shit with unrecognisable vocals and a soundscape that might have had cowbells and pan flutes.

'I'm going over to Bear's later,' she said. 'After his shift at the pub.'

Hesse's brain ticked over. 'What time?' he asked, as casually as he could.

She turned to look at him. 'You know I can read you like a book, don't you?'

'What do you mean? I was just asking what time you'd be going to Bear's place.'

'What's Fenna up to tonight?' she asked.

He shrugged. 'I dunno. I haven't heard from her since this morning.'

'But she might come over tonight, huh?'

'Mum! Come on. I haven't spoken to her, all right.'

'Are you two sleeping together?'

He dropped the knife he was using. 'No!'

'But you're thinking about it. Just remember the two Cs, young man.'

'I know. Contraception and consent. You've been telling me that since before I even knew what they were. Besides, we're both adults.'

'You're seventeen, Hesse. You're not an adult. And neither is Fenna.'

When dinner was ready, they ate together in the kitchen. Thankfully, the conversation veered away from sex as they returned to the events of the weekend. By the time they were finished, Hesse's head was spinning, not so much at what had happened—that couldn't be changed—but by what would be expected of him now.

'Rachel has already asked me to speak at the Strike for Climate rally in Castlereagh next month,' he said. 'But the principal said she'd suspend anybody who went.'

'You have to make up your own mind, Hesse. What's more important to you?'

'Aren't you supposed to be the responsible parent and tell me I can't miss a day of school for a rally?'

'Yes. But I'm also being a responsible parent if I encourage you to stand up for what's right.'

After dinner, Imogen spent ages getting changed, then stood before him while he washed the dishes. 'What do you think?' she asked.

She'd put on a pair of slim-fit jeans and a top he hadn't seen before. Her hair was brushed back off her face and she was wearing make-up, a rarity for her. She held a small bag.

'Pretty good, I reckon,' he said.

'I might stay overnight,' she said, pulling the bag onto her shoulder. 'You'll be okay?'

Hesse knew there was a lot going unsaid in this conversation. 'Sure,' he said.

'Just remember, you've got school tomorrow.' She arched her eyebrows. 'And so has Fenna.' She kissed him on the cheek, grabbed her car keys off the bench and walked out the front door.

Hesse went to his room to get his phone. On the bedside table, under his lamp, Imogen had left a packet of condoms. He shook his head and smiled.

He messaged Fenna, asking if she could come over, making a point of mentioning Imogen was out for the night. It took a few minutes for her to respond: *Okay*

Then another message arrived from the mystery texter: *Are you coming or not?*

It was nearly eight. It would take him five minutes to get to the boatshed. His curiosity had got the better of him. Besides, he could get close and just watch for a while. He knew all the tracks along the river and was confident he could get away quickly if it was a set-up.

He locked the house and, with the memory of the brick attack still fresh in his mind, cautiously wheeled his bike out onto the road. The street was deserted. Pedalling quickly and without a light, he sped down Russell Street. At the bridge he turned into the darkness of the river track. When he got within twenty metres of the shed, he slid off his bike and hid it in the bush. Then he circled around until he had a clear view of the shed. Waiting in the tea trees, he checked his phone was on silent. There was a message from Fenna: *9.30.*

His heart pounded so hard he was sure anyone within half a kilomtere would hear it.

There was no movement around the shed. A car swept by on the other side of the river, its headlights catching the front window of the surf shop, illuminating it for an instant. His legs were cramping up in the cold and he wished he'd worn a warmer jacket. The wind was light but it had turned onshore in the afternoon and now the cool ocean air was sweeping up the valley.

After about ten minutes he heard the rattle of an approaching bike. He held his breath and watched. The rider dismounted and leaned the bike against the side of the shed, looking around warily. They hesitated for a few seconds then pulled the piece of iron aside and stepped through.

He moved closer to the shed. With his face to the wall he said, 'Who's there?'

'Hesse? Is that you?' came a reply. It was Felicity.

He pulled out his phone and turned on the torch before pushing the sheet aside and squeezing through.

Felicity stood near the side wall, with her arm up shielding her eyes from the torch. 'Hey,' she said. 'Thanks for coming. I need to talk to you.'

Hesse leaned his back against the opposite wall and crossed his arms. 'Okay, I'm listening.'

'I sent the envelope,' she said.

'Yeah, I guessed that much,' Hesse replied. 'What I can't work out is why?'

She turned away and wiped at her face.

'It doesn't matter why. The main thing is the figures are genuine. Hadron has been lying about its emissions for years.'

'We're having them checked out by some lawyers in Melbourne.'

'The emissions are only part of the story.'

'What do you mean?'

'Hadron has hushed up so many things, accidents, spills into the river. You remember that fish kill last year, the one they said was because of low oxygen levels in the water?'

'That was Hadron?'

She nodded. 'The worst thing, though, are the filters.'

'Filters?' Hesse was racing to keep up.

'Before it was allowed to expand the mine and increase production four years ago the EPA made it install industrial filters in the smokestack. They cost Hadron millions.'

'And?'

'The filters never worked properly. But the parent company in Texas decided they were too expensive to replace.' She pulled a piece of paper from her pocket, unfolded it and handed it to Hesse. 'It's a screenshot of an email,' she said.

'What were the filters supposed to do?'

'Catch most of the sulphur dioxide before it was emitted.'

'Into the air we breathe.'

'Now you're catching on.'

'And that's why Hadron has changed the emission figures.'

'Like I said, the figures I gave you are real. This,' she said, pointing to the piece of paper, 'is the proof you need to force the EPA to inspect the filters.' Felicity was speaking as though she was out of breath. Or terrified of what she was doing.

Something wasn't stacking up for Hesse. 'Why didn't you give me this yesterday, with the other sheets?'

'I wanted to see how it played out at the meeting. This is the last piece of the jigsaw, Hesse. The power station will be shut down if this comes out.'

Hesse pressed back against the wall. 'I still don't get it,' he said. 'Your dad's going to be blamed. He could end up in jail.'

She had turned away from him, but he saw a little shudder in her shoulders.

'Are you okay?' he asked.

She sniffed. 'Just cold,' she said. 'I gotta go.' She moved to duck through the gap at the back then hesitated and stood up. 'Thanks for asking, though.' She leaned in and kissed him on the cheek. Then she was gone. Hesse heard the bike rattle away towards the bridge.

He waited for a while, digesting what had just happened. The information was huge, but all he could think of was Felicity and why she had betrayed her father.

Eventually, he stepped outside and slid the sheet of iron back into place. It was colder still on the ride home. The first flecks of rain hit him in the face as he turned into his street and started to climb the hill. He hoped it wouldn't get too heavy. Fenna might think twice about coming over if it was raining.

The house was warm, but the fire was burning low, so he added another log. The smell of dinner hung in the kitchen and the rain beat heavier on the roof.

He flattened out the sheet of paper Felicity had given him, photographed it with his phone and sent it to Ruby. She'd know what to do with it.

Then he tidied his bedroom, throwing dirty clothes into the wardrobe and sliding the door shut. He sniffed under his armpits and decided a quick shower was a good idea. It was only ten past nine and as much as anything, he wanted to suck up some time, which was now moving at glacial speed. After his shower he applied liberal amounts of deodorant and ran some gel through his hair.

Back in the lounge room, he opened the cupboard at the bottom of the dresser and took out a bottle of vodka. He poured himself a glass and was just about to down it when there was a knock at the front door.

Fenna stood on the porch, drenched. Her hair was matted and her whole body was shaking. 'What do you think?' she asked, spreading her arms and turning her hands up. 'It's my drowned-rat look.'

Hesse directed her to the fire. She was wearing Imogen's jacket and it was soaked. She took it off and Hesse hung it on the back of a chair. Her clothes clung to her body. 'Could you make me a warm drink?' she asked.

'Sure.' Hesse was even more nervous now she was here, so the distraction was welcome. He put some milk with Milo in the microwave. When he turned back Fenna was standing against the glow of the fire, steam rising from her jeans.

'What's been happening?' she asked. Hesse listened for any waver in her voice, any clue she might not be coping tonight. He was beginning to read her a little better. There was an edge to her voice, but she seemed confident enough.

'Just the usual,' he said. 'I'm all over the internet, I was on the news tonight and I now have fifty thousand followers on Twitter.'

She leaned towards the fire and brushed her fingers through her hair to dry it. 'I saw the news,' she said. 'I thought you were great. Aunt Lydia isn't your number-one fan, though. She thinks you should keep quiet and let the adults sort it out.'

'Now, there's a surprise,' he said.

When the microwave pinged he took the cup out, but then hesitated. 'Are you sure you don't want something stronger?' he asked, pointing to the vodka bottle on the sink.

She smiled. 'Only if you're having one.'

As he poured another shot, he felt himself starting to sweat. He hoped the deodorant was working.

'Cheers,' he said, handing her a glass.

'*Proost*,' she replied, and sculled it.

They stood side by side in front of the fire.

'I had the strangest thing happen tonight,' Hesse said. He told her about the mystery text and the meeting with Felicity.

Fenna didn't seem surprised. 'You know what?' she said when he'd finished. 'I get strange vibes from her, like there's a different person underneath trying to get out. Remember when we saw her in the library last week? I don't think it was

Shakespeare that was upsetting her.'

'What do you reckon could be going on?' he asked. 'And why would she expose her dad like that?'

Fenna turned to look at him. 'Who knows?' she said. 'Every family has secrets.'

This conversation wasn't getting Hesse any closer to the romantic night he'd planned. He placed his glass carefully on the mantel over the fireplace. 'Remember what you said this morning,' he began. 'About, you know...'

'No, I don't remember. About what?'

'When we were riding down the hill?'

She shook her head. '*Nee*. I still can't remember.' She put her glass next to his.

'You said we should have sex.' He blurted it out quicker than he would have liked.

She nodded. 'Ah, now I remember. I think I also said, some time.'

'You said soon.'

'*Ja*, but soon can mean next week, next month.' She tilted her head and he saw the smile creasing her lips.

'Or tonight,' he said.

'Tonight would be *very* soon.'

Hesse hadn't expected to have to play this game. She was the one who'd suggested it, not him.

Maybe she saw the uncertainty in his face. She turned to him, put her hands on his hips and drew him closer. The flickering firelight lit her face as she kissed him softly on the lips. 'Give me a minute,' she breathed, taking him by the shoulders and pointing towards his bedroom. 'Wait in there.'

Hesse sat on the bed and switched on the bedside lamp. Then he turned it off. Then on, then off again.

He waited and listened. He heard the faint rustle of clothes and he imagined Fenna undressing by the fire. But then, the creak of the front door and the quiet click as it shut.

Hesse jumped off the bed and ran down the hallway. When he opened the door, the fine rain swept in.

Fenna was gone.

17

Hesse was woken by banging at the door. He fumbled for his phone to check the time: *12.06*. He turned on the lamp, rolled out of bed and threw on his trackpants. The banging stopped when he switched on the hall light.

'Fenna?' a woman's voice called.

Then a man. 'Come on, Hesse. We know she's there.'

Hesse opened the door to find Colin and Julie Turner huddled against the cold.

'This is just not on, Hesse,' Julie said, pushing past him. 'Fenna!' she shouted.

Hesse was confused. Fenna had left hours ago. He'd tried to call her but her phone had rung out so he'd messaged her instead, telling her everything was okay. He knew she'd be feeling bad about having done a runner and he wanted to reassure her.

'She's not here,' he said.

'Rubbish!' Julie said. 'She's a liar, that girl. She's done nothing but deceive us since she arrived.' She marched down the hallway looking into Imogen's room, then Hesse's.

Colin had stepped inside and shut the front door. 'Come on, Julie. That's not fair,' he called after her. He seemed calmer than his wife so Hesse turned to him.

'She left ages ago,' he said. 'After we finished our homework.'

Hesse saw the concern on Colin's face.

'Hasn't she come home?' Hesse asked.

'She said she'd be home by ten-thirty,' Colin said.

'On a school night!' Julie called from Hesse's room. 'Honestly, Colin, why you'd even let her, I've got no idea.' She emerged from his room holding the packet of condoms. 'Where's your mother?' she demanded.

Hesse was torn between embarrassment at the condoms and anger at Julie's badgering. 'Mum's not here,' he said.

'Obviously!' she snorted. 'You'd better call her.'

'Hang on,' Hesse said. 'What about Fenna? If she didn't come home, where is she?'

Colin edged between Hesse and his wife. 'Seriously, Hesse, is she here?'

'No, she's not. She left at about ten. Have you tried ringing her?'

'Of course we have,' Julie said. She dropped the condoms on the sideboard. 'Wait until your mother sees those,' she added.

'And that,' pointing at the vodka bottle.

'We need to call the police,' Colin said, ignoring her.

Hesse's mind was racing. He hadn't told anyone about the spotlight incident, and he guessed Fenna hadn't either. What if she'd been followed tonight? What if they had waited until she was riding home? He kicked himself for not having gone after her. He checked his phone for messages again. Nothing. Then he tried calling her, but it went straight to message bank.

Colin dialled triple zero.

Meanwhile, Hesse rang Imogen. He had to try twice before she picked up. 'Hesse?' she said, her voice heavy with sleep. 'What is it? What's happened?'

He explained as best he could. Julie hovered over him looking as though she might snatch the phone from him at any second.

'I'm on my way,' Imogen said.

Fifteen minutes later she arrived with Bear. The Turners had calmed down a little and Hesse had made them cups of tea. He wanted to go looking for Fenna but the police had said to stay put until they got there.

Hesse filled Imogen and Bear in on what had happened. He stuck to the story about doing homework.

Julie got up to retrieve the condoms from the sideboard in the lounge room but Hesse had already put them away. That didn't stop her, though. 'They were sleeping together!' she said to Imogen. 'Where were you while all this was going on?'

Imogen had picked up the vibe in the room as soon as she'd arrived. 'Excuse me,' she said. 'But as far as I remember this is my house, not yours. And as for Hesse and Fenna, I trust them to have done the right thing.'

'The right thing!' A red flush had crept up Julie's neck and it was now taking over her face. 'As if they are going to do the right thing when there are no adults around.'

Colin stayed quiet. Hesse guessed it was his default position when his wife was upset.

The argument could have become more heated but they were interrupted by the arrival of Sergeant Howard. He looked as though he had dressed in the dark. His tie was crooked and he'd missed a button on his jacket.

'All right,' he said. 'Let's not panic. In ninety-nine per cent of these cases there's been some sort of misunderstanding and the missing person comes home of their own accord.'

Hesse didn't like Howard but he wanted to believe him.

'Now, young man,' the cop began. 'Colin told me what's happened but I'd like to hear it from you.'

Hesse recounted the events of the night again, sticking to the homework story and leaving out the suddenness of Fenna's departure.

'So, she left here at ten and as far as you know she was going straight home?' Howard asked Hesse.

'That's right,' he said.

'Was she upset when she left?' Howard asked.

'No.'

She hadn't been upset. He knew she'd just changed her mind or panicked and decided to go home.

'So, you hadn't argued about anything? No disagreements?'

Hesse could see where this was going. 'No!' he said.

'Is there anywhere else she might have gone?' Colin asked. 'A place you've been before?'

Hesse thought of the boatshed but he couldn't see any reason she'd go there. He shook his head.

Howard turned to Imogen. 'Do you think this is linked in any way to the incident yesterday?' he asked. 'With the brick.'

'I hope not, Sergeant,' Imogen answered.

'There is something else,' Hesse said. He knew he should have told his mum about the spotlight incident but it had been forgotten in the excitement of the day. He took a deep breath and recounted what had happened the night before.

'A weapon was discharged!' Howard was aghast. 'In town! And you didn't think to report it?'

'There's been so much happening,' Hesse said. He knew it was a weak excuse. He registered the shock on everyone's faces. Imogen's eyes widened.

'I'm pretty sure he shot into the air,' Hesse said.

'*Pretty* sure?' Howard asked. 'How would you know if it was dark?'

Colin interrupted, 'This isn't helping us find Fenna.'

Howard huffed and asked Hesse if he recognised either of the men.

'The one with the rifle, I'm pretty sure it was a bloke called Stanton. He works for Hadron and he's hassled me before.' He turned to Imogen. 'He was the one that took my photo up at the fence a couple of weeks ago.'

'And what about the car?' Howard continued.

'I can't be sure. It was too far away.'

'Do you know any other people in town who have'—he hesitated, looking for the right words—'shown an interest in Fenna?'

'Only Jago Crothers,' Hesse replied. 'He took her for a surf lesson, but she cut it short.'

'Why was that?' The cop leaned forward. Hesse guessed he knew Jago pretty well.

'Fenna didn't feel comfortable and she left.'

This was obviously news to the Turners. They exchanged glances.

'All right,' Howard said. 'If there's nothing else, we'll wait until morning. In all likelihood she'll have come home by then. I'll speak to Stanton. The incident by the river might not be related to Fenna going missing.'

'There is one more thing,' Hesse said. He felt he was betraying Fenna as soon as he opened his mouth, but he needed to tell them. He looked at the table as he spoke. 'She freaks out sometimes. She gets anxious and has panic attacks.'

Howard sat down again. 'Did you know about this?' he asked the Turners.

Julie shook her head, but Colin spoke. 'She's on medication for anxiety,' he said, calmly. 'She didn't tell me, but I saw the packet in her bag. It's nothing unusual. I'm a pharmacist. You'd be surprised how many people in town are on those sorts of meds.'

'And you didn't think to tell me?' Julie said, shaking her head.

'The girl's got a right to privacy,' he replied.

Hesse was warming to Colin Turner.

Howard was looking at Hesse again. 'Was there anything that happened between you two that might have caused her anxiety?'

It was a loaded question. 'She left quickly,' he said. 'We didn't argue or anything. She just said she had to go.'

'So, she freaked out about something?' Howard asked. The words sounded strange coming from him.

'No, not really. Sometimes she can't explain, she just has to get out of a situation.'

Colin was nodding. 'Don't read too much into that, Sergeant,' he said. 'It's a coping mechanism. The smallest thing can trigger it.'

Howard didn't seem convinced but he pushed to his feet again and tucked his notebook into his pocket. 'Nothing else, Hesse?' he asked pointedly, frustrated at the drip-feeding of information. 'Nothing you can think of that might give us a clue where she could be?'

'No.'

'I suggest we all get some sleep, then,' Howard said. 'If she hasn't come home by morning we'll get Castlereagh involved. Make some more enquiries. Organise a search.'

After Howard and the Turners had left, Hesse tried Fenna's phone, but it rang through to message bank again. It was one in the morning, but he was wide awake.

Imogen and Bear didn't look as though they were going to bed any time soon either. Bear was on his second coffee.

'I need to go and look for her,' Hesse said.

'Where, Hesse?' Imogen asked. 'Is there something you didn't tell Howard?'

'No, but it's better than lying awake all night worrying.'

Bear held up his car keys. 'Let's go,' he said.

Imogen stood up. 'I'm coming too.'

The rain had moved on but the wind was bitter. Bear had an old Toyota troopie with spotlights mounted on the bull bar. They drove along the river, the same route Hesse had taken with Fenna the night before. Hesse got out of the car where the track veered away into the scrub closer to the bank. He used the torch on his phone to peer into darker spaces off the track, looking for a glint of metal that might be a bike. Meanwhile, Imogen and Bear drove ahead, checking the road, before turning around and coming back towards him.

Finding nothing, they tried a different route. The pub was dark inside apart from the glow of the poker machines in the gaming room. They did a lap of the empty car park before following Camp Road to the bottom of Fenna's street. The lights were still on at the Turner place, but they'd agreed to ring Hesse if she arrived home.

They stopped to think for a minute, the low rumble of the big diesel the only sound they could hear on a freezing Tuesday morning in Shelbourne.

'Hesse?' Imogen said. 'Remember that first night you met Fenna at Haystacks? Why was she out there?'

'I never asked,' he replied, 'but it's worth a look.'

The Toyota slaved up the steep hill out of town before the road levelled off heading west. The asphalt glowed from the rain and the white lines shone in the headlights. They swung off the road into the Haystacks car park, the wide stretch of gravel sloping down towards a couple of picnic tables and the platform overlooking the beach. Hesse got out and checked the area, calling Fenna's name above the rattling wind. He ran down the track to the beach, but he knew he would have seen her bike if she was there.

'Let's try Corrals,' he said, climbing back into the car.

Branches scraped the sides as Bear manoeuvred the troopie down the track to the sandy clearing where Hesse and Fenna had left their bikes the previous afternoon. Bear swung around in the tight space between the overhanging trees. The beam of the headlights was broken up by the coastal scrub.

He had barely straightened up when Hesse called out. 'Stop. Back there.'

He pointed to a track on their left. Bear turned the troopie again and switched on the spotlights. There was a car. Most of it was screened by the trees, but the back number plate reflected in their lights. Without warning, it revved loudly and reversed hard towards them. At the last second the driver swung the wheel violently, sending a cloud of sand into air. For an instant it stopped next to them.

'That's Jago's ute,' Hesse said.

He could see through the back window. There was someone in the passenger seat and they were thrashing around, punching at the driver. As quickly as it had come to a halt, the ute accelerated and fishtailed towards the road, side-swiping a tree as the driver wrestled for control.

Bear reacted quickly, planting his foot and taking off after it. The big four-wheel drive handled the sand more easily and he gained ground before the ute made it out onto Ocean Road and hurtled towards town. The troopie was at a disadvantage on the bitumen, slow and lumbering, but Bear ground through the gears and picked up speed. They were a hundred metres behind Jago when they reached the sixty zone coming into Shelbourne.

Imogen reached across and gripped Bear's arm. 'Take it easy,' she said. 'We know who it is. We can call the cops and let them do the chasing.'

'But Fenna,' Hesse yelled above the engine noise.

Bear glanced at him in the rear-view mirror, then eased off the accelerator as they dropped down the hill towards the Fat Controller. They could see the tail-lights of Jago's ute ahead of them. He wasn't slowing down. He was at the bridge by the time they came around the bend and straightened out along the river.

Imogen fumbled for the phone in her jacket pocket. Its screen lit her face as she keyed triple zero.

They heard a loud bang, like an explosion, as they approached the bridge.

'Police, please,' Imogen said. She looked up when Bear hit the brakes hard at the roundabout in front of the shops. 'No, wait,' she said. 'Ambulance.'

Bear pulled to the side of the road and switched off the motor.

Hesse leaned forward and tried to make sense of what he was seeing. A give-way sign was bent at the base and flattened to the ground and a muddy swathe had been cut through the grass in the middle of the roundabout. On the other side, the ute was buckled around a power pole, steam and smoke spewing from the engine. Glass and metal littered the road and glistened in the orange streetlights.

For a few seconds they sat where they were, stunned. Hesse was the first to move, jumping out the back door and feeling the rush of the cold night air. For reasons he didn't understand, he couldn't run. His feet seemed anchored to the road. Bile lifted in his throat and he forced it back down. Bear was already halfway across the roundabout while Imogen walked more slowly, giving directions to the ambulance as she went.

Finally, Hesse was able to move and he caught up with them. The mud of the roundabout stuck to their shoes as they neared the ute.

'Careful,' Bear said, grabbing Hesse by the arm.

The engine hissed and pinged. They approached from the back, dreading what they might find. Hesse's heart leaped into his mouth when he saw the mangled frame of Fenna's bike protruding from the ute's tray. Then his eyes were drawn to a shape on the grass on the other side of the road barrier. He touched Imogen's arm and pointed. She nodded and stepped over the barrier, then bent low to see the face.

'Jago,' she said quietly.

Once Hesse heard that, he swung back to the wreck. The driver's side had taken the full impact of the pole, wrapping the cabin into a jagged V-shape. He moved to the passenger side and tried to open the door. It was jammed shut so he climbed onto the buckled bonnet, feeling the heat of the engine against his jeans. Through the shattered windscreen he saw Fenna slumped forward with her head on the dashboard, blood and glass everywhere.

'Mum,' Hesse yelled. 'Here. She's here.' He hardly recognised his own voice, it was so broken and high-pitched.

Imogen was tending to Jago but Bear climbed up onto the bonnet next to him.

Hesse leaned into the cabin and gently touched Fenna's shoulder.

'Fenna,' he said. 'Fenna!'

She didn't respond.

'I don't think we should move her, mate,' Bear said.

Something in Hesse's head was struggling to the surface—something he should remember. His brain was frozen in the moment but he pushed past it and seized on the word. *Airway,* he remembered from the first-aid course he'd done at school.

'She's gotta be able to breathe,' he said loudly.

'Carefully, then,' Bear said.

Bear's huge frame seemed to be taking up all the space so Hesse pushed further into the cabin. The glass at the edge of the windscreen tore at his jacket. He cupped her face in his hands and, supporting her neck, gently eased her back in the seat until her head was upright. He couldn't tell if she was breathing or not.

More than anything in that moment he wanted her to open her eyes, to recognise him, to tell him she was okay. But her eyes remained closed. There was a deep red mark across one side of her neck where the seatbelt had dug into her skin. He fumbled two fingers around to the other side of her neck and checked for a pulse. He thought he found it but it disappeared just as quickly. Sliding one hand down the side of her body he felt the warm stickiness of blood.

Tears welled in his eyes and fell onto her lap.

There were more lights now. Another car had stopped. Low voices.

Hesse's face was inches from Fenna's. Still holding her head with one hand, he gently brushed the hair back from her cheek with the other. Her skin was cold. It seemed impossible that only a couple of hours ago this same girl had pulled him close and kissed him in front of the fire.

He didn't know how long he had held her but he was vaguely aware of more people arriving. Imogen leaned over the bonnet and wrapped a reassuring arm around his waist. Someone levered the door open with a crowbar. It gave way with a groan and the cabin filled with torchlight. Fenna's face glowed a hollow white. She still hadn't moved. Another pair of hands reached in and took over the cradling of her head. Hesse's body ached with the cold and the sharp pain of metal and glass digging into him, but he didn't want to leave her.

Then he heard a low moan. Her eyes flickered for an instant and then closed again.

The air was split by the sound of sirens and the night erupted with the flashing of red and blue lights. Someone tugged at Hesse's belt, pulling him away from Fenna. He resisted but then felt hands on his arms, lifting him away from the wreck as the paramedics moved in. Imogen guided him and sat him down on the guardrail, her arm firmly around his shoulder.

Bear sat on the other side.

'Will she be okay?' Hesse asked, knowing they wouldn't have an answer.

'They're doing everything they can for her, Hesse,' Imogen said.

'I heard her try to say something,' he said.

Imogen pulled him closer.

'Jago?' Hesse asked.

'He's not good,' she said.

Hesse looked to where Jago lay. Two paramedics knelt either side of him, the ground strewn with bloodied swabs and bandages. One, a woman Hesse recognised from the campaign meetings, was doing chest compressions while the other held a mask over Jago's nose and mouth. He could hear her counting, 'Twenty-eight, twenty-nine, thirty. Breath. Breath.'

Hesse was cold and numb. He shuddered.

'We should go,' Imogen said. 'We're just in the way here.'

Two paramedics were with Fenna, one leaning in the door and the other reaching through the broken windscreen. Hesse looked up to see a policewoman standing beside him.

'Which of you is the driver of the troopie?' she asked.

'Me,' Bear replied.

'And you witnessed the accident?'

'No,' he said. 'We arrived just after it had happened.'

Turning to Imogen, she said, 'Why did you ask for the police before the ambulance?'

'We were following them,' Imogen said.

'Why?' the policewoman asked, her voice turning from sympathetic to inquisitive.

'We think Fenna, the girl in the ute, had been abducted.'

'So you know the couple in the car?' she asked.

They're not a couple, Hesse felt like saying.

'Yes,' Imogen responded.

Now she turned her gaze on Bear. 'Were you chasing the ute, sir?'

'No,' he said emphatically. 'We'd slowed down. We were following at a safe distance.'

'How fast were you going across the bridge?'

'I was doing sixty,' he replied.

She looked back at the troopie for a second as though she might find answers to her questions there. 'Can I see your licence please, sir?'

After she had taken their details and asked a dozen more questions, she told them to go home. She instructed Bear to come to the Shelbourne police station first thing in the morning to make a statement. Imogen and Hesse would be called in if they were needed.

Before they left, they watched Fenna being lifted out of the ute. An oxygen mask covered her mouth and nose, there were tubes in her arms and her body was wrapped in a foil sheet. She was placed on a stretcher and wheeled towards the ambulance.

The last thing Hesse saw before they retreated to the troopie was a blanket being placed over Jago's body, covering his face.

18

Back at home, Hesse couldn't get the image of Fenna being lifted from the ute out of his head. Slowly, the adrenaline that had been keeping him on high alert seeped away, leaving him drained. Imogen made tea and they stared at each over the table.

'We should get our story straight,' Bear said. 'About how it happened.'

'There's only one story,' Imogen said. 'We were out looking for Fenna.'

'We were chasing them,' Bear said.

'No.' Imogen was emphatic. 'You slowed down, remember? We were following them. That's all. This wasn't our fault.'

Bear shook his head. 'That's not how it feels.'

Hesse was hardly listening to the conversation. His mind

was still back at the scene of the accident, his hands holding Fenna, whispering to her, telling her she'd be okay, to hold on, to breathe.

'You need to go to bed,' Imogen said.

His head was a fog, but he registered his mum's concern.

'Okay,' he said.

'We'll be here if you need us,' she said.

Every part of his body was stiff as he shuffled towards the bathroom. When he looked in the mirror there was a smear of blood on his cheek. He washed it away and cleaned his teeth.

'Please,' he whispered to his reflection, 'let her be okay.' He'd never been religious, but if by some chance there was a god, he was willing, for Fenna's sake, to ask for help.

He hauled off his clothes in the bedroom, leaving them where they dropped, and climbed into bed. Then he picked up the jumper he'd been wearing when he and Fenna had held each other in front of the fire. He wanted desperately to smell Fenna there. He knew he was imagining it but he thought there was the faintest scent of her on the fabric, something he recognised but couldn't put his finger on, shampoo maybe or deodorant. He buried his face in it.

He woke early and checked his phone. There were messages from Jake, Mus, Theo, Ruby and even Felicity. They all said pretty much the same thing: *Stay strong, she'll be okay*

But they hadn't seen the mangled wreck. They hadn't seen the blood and the tubes and the masks or felt the bite of broken glass. They hadn't seen Jago's body under a blanket.

Out in the kitchen, Bear was in his customary position at the stove cooking breakfast. The smell of the food stirred Hesse's stomach and he realised how hungry he was.

Imogen was sitting where she'd been last night and he wondered if she'd slept at all. She looked up at him and half-smiled, half-grimaced.

'Any news?' he asked.

'Fenna's going to be okay,' Imogen said, her voice both tired and relieved.

Hesse felt his legs buckle under him. He gripped the table and slumped into a chair. It was like he had been holding his breath for an eternity and now he could breathe again.

'The hospital's not saying much,' Imogen continued, 'but Col Turner is with her. I've spoken to him this morning. They did a heap of scans and X-rays in emergency. She's fractured four ribs, punctured a lung and she has lots of bruising and lacerations. And concussion. She's very lucky.'

'She's smart,' Bear said, placing a plate stacked with toast, eggs and tomato in front of Hesse.

'What do you mean?' Hesse asked.

'She had her seatbelt on. Jago didn't. That's why she's alive and he's not.'

There was a knock at the front door. Imogen walked slowly down the hall. 'Just leave your bags on the porch,' Hesse heard her say.

Mus and Jake came nervously into the kitchen, Jake having to duck to get under the doorframe. They were in their school uniforms, Mus with a scarf around his neck.

'We were on our way to the bus,' Jake said. 'Wanted to check how you were.'

Imogen told them about Fenna.

'She'll be okay then?' Jake asked.

'Eventually,' Imogen said.

'You blokes want a cup of tea or something?' Bear asked. 'Toast? Bacon?'

'No, thanks,' Jake said.

Hesse could have told Bear they were both Muslim, but he held back.

'Thanks for dropping by,' Hesse said, getting up. Mus gave him an awkward hug and a couple of hefty slaps on the back. Jake was more formal. He held out his hand and Hesse shook it. Only two days ago Jake's parents had stood in this same kitchen and begged him not to speak at the meeting.

'Are you coming to school?' Mus asked, looking relieved to have got the hug out of the way.

'Not today,' Imogen said to Hesse. 'You need to rest. And we'll see if Fenna can have visitors.'

Hesse hadn't even thought about school. He could imagine the news spreading like a bushfire. There'd be all sorts of wild theories about why Fenna was in the car with Jago and how the accident had happened. At least Jake and Mus could let them know how she was doing.

The boys had to get to the bus. 'Call us if you need anything,' Mus said.

After they'd left Hesse finished his breakfast and leaned back in his chair, rubbing his hands on his thighs. He took the folded sheet of paper that Felicity had given him out of his pocket and showed it to Imogen and Bear.

They read it together.

'Incredible,' Bear said. 'We need to send this to Ruby.'

'I already have,' Hesse said.

The morning passed in a blur of phone calls and messages. Ruby and Oliver wanted to know the source of the screenshot email, but Hesse told them it was another anonymous drop in his letterbox. They had released it to the media. Shelbourne was centre stage right now and they had to strike before the news cycle moved on.

By midday the news that Hadron had provided false information to the regulator was leading the online news sites. Twitter exploded with the information. Hesse was relieved the focus had shifted from him to Oliver and Ruby. His followers had grown by another five thousand overnight, but he hardly took any notice. Felicity's dad was nowhere to be seen on the news and Hesse wondered what her family would be going through. The Hadron people who fronted the cameras were dressed in smart suits and spoke earnestly of how shocked they were at the revelations. The environment minister was questioned in parliament about how this could have happened on her watch.

Hesse allowed all the news to wash over him. He didn't care anymore. He just wanted to see Fenna. Bear had gone to the police station to give a statement so it was just him and Imogen left to clean up the dishes and lose themselves in the silence. Hesse washed and Imogen dried. He took his time with each plate, liking the feeling of his hands in the warm water.

'Are you okay?' Imogen asked.

He pressed his hands into the bottom of the sink and watched the soap bubbles around his wrists. 'Honestly, Mum, I don't know,' he said. 'It's like the world sped up while I wasn't looking and now I'm struggling to hang on.'

She wrapped her arm around his waist, just like she did when they'd sat on the guardrail after the accident, just like she'd been doing for as long as he could remember.

'How do you feel about Jago?' she asked.

'I didn't like him, but he didn't deserve to die. He wasn't much older than me.'

She kissed him on the shoulder.

'I feel like I've been making it up as I go along,' he said. 'I hardly get a breath before the next catastrophe happens.'

She smiled. 'Welcome to adult life.'

'Yesterday you told me I wasn't an adult,' he said.

'I think there've been a few things happen in the last twenty-four hours that have changed that. Doing your *homework* with Fenna, for example.'

Hesse swished his hands in the sink. 'It didn't work out last night,' he said.

'You didn't pressure her, I hope.'

'No. I would never do that.'

She nodded. 'Maybe she just wasn't ready.'

Castlereagh Hospital was a hotchpotch of old and new buildings connected by covered walkways. Imogen worked there so she was able to pull some strings. They were allowed to see Fenna for fifteen minutes, and only one person at a time. She was in a shared ward with five other beds. The corridor smelled of antiseptic and meat stew.

Imogen let Hesse go first.

He hardly recognised Fenna when the nurse pulled the curtain back. Her bed was by the window and weak sunlight fell across her face. One eye was swollen shut. She had a small row of stitches along her hairline and tiny cuts on her cheek and chin. The rest of her body was hidden under a loose-fitting gown and her hands lay on top of the sheet, dark bruising around her wrists. A tube ran out one side of the gown and there was a low, bubbling noise as she breathed.

'*Hai*,' she mumbled when she saw him.

Tears filled Hesse's eyes but he quickly blinked them away. He sat on the chair by the bed and she reached for his hand.

'Hey,' he said. 'How are you feeling?'

'Like shit,' she said, trying to smile. 'How do I look?'

'Beautiful,' he replied.

She tried to laugh but grabbed at her chest.

'Sorry,' he said.

She threaded her fingers through his and squeezed. 'It's so good to see you,' she said.

'Do you remember anything about last night?' he asked, keeping his voice low.

'I'm so sorry I ran out,' she said.

'It's okay,' he said. 'Really.'

'I don't know what I was thinking. I wanted to be with you, I really did.'

Hesse shifted a little closer and cautiously stroked her shoulder. 'What about the accident?' he asked.

She turned away. 'I don't remember everything. It's coming back in flashes,' she said.

'That'd be the concussion. Have you spoken to the police yet?'

It was barely a whisper. 'No.'

'Has anyone told you about Jago?'

She nodded. 'Colin.'

She pushed back against the pillows and tried to catch her breath. 'Can you help me sit up?' she asked.

Hesse slid his arm behind her, feeling the warm skin of her back where the gown was loosely tied. Fenna pressed down with her hands and groaned as Hesse lifted her so she was sitting up a bit.

'My parents are coming over,' she said. 'As soon as I'm well enough they're taking me home.'

Something in Hesse's head told him this was inevitable. He had finally found a girl who understood him in a way no one else did, and now she was going to be taken away. He tried not to think of what his life would be like without her.

'What happened after you left my place?' he asked.

Fenna took her time to answer, as though she was trying to get the order of events right in her own head. 'I think he was waiting outside,' she began. 'He might have followed me there.'

Her breath became wheezy again and the bubbling noise from the tube increased.

A nurse stuck her head around the corner of the curtain. 'Are you all right, Fenna?' she asked.

'*Ja.*'

'Just a few more minutes, then,' the nurse said, and her rubber-soled shoes squeaked away towards the corridor.

'I have to tell you something,' Fenna said, pulling Hesse closer. She was rocking gently backwards and forwards like she needed to coax the words out. 'It was my fault,' she whispered.

'What do you mean? Did you get into the car with him?'

'No, of course not!' She paused, struggling for breath. 'He knocked me off my bike and dragged me into his car.'

'So, it's not your fault.'

She shook her head. More wheezing.

'It's okay,' Hesse said. 'We don't have to talk about it now. I'll come in tomorrow. You can tell me then.'

But she pulled at his wrist. 'I caused the accident,' she said. 'I grabbed the steering wheel.' She squeezed his arm tighter, waiting for a reaction.

Hesse took a few seconds to process what she'd said. 'He'd abducted you, Fenna,' he said firmly. 'Of course you'd try and do something. Anyone would.'

'But he's dead!' she said.

Hesse struggled to stay calm. 'I know, but that's not your fault. If he hadn't taken you, he wouldn't have been speeding and he wouldn't have lost control.'

Fenna slumped back onto the pillows and looked at the ceiling. 'Should I tell the police?' she asked.

'That's up to you,' Hesse said. 'But you don't need to. No one needs to know.'

'I know,' she said.

Imogen was quiet on the way home. She'd only had a couple of minutes with Fenna before they'd had to leave. The paddocks sped by in a blur. The Castlereagh–Shelbourne Road cut through the last remaining farmland that hadn't been eaten up by the new estates spreading towards the coast. The news came on the car radio at four o'clock and Hadron led the bulletin.

The Hadron Corporation has agreed to a State Government demand for the immediate suspension of work at its open-cut coalmine and power station at Shelbourne, on Victoria's west coast. Leaked documents have allegedly revealed Hadron has been flouting the state's laws on emissions. The manager of the Shelbourne facility, Terrence Holden, has been stood down pending an EPA enquiry. Police have not ruled out criminal charges.

In a statement released this morning Hadron said the company would cooperate fully with any inquiry. The company's shares fell heavily in early trading, dropping thirty per cent on local markets.

Libby Bannister is the mayor of the West Coast Shire. 'Shelbourne will be hit hard by this news. Eighty workers could lose their jobs. It's been a tough twenty-four hours for the town. A popular young local man was killed in a tragic car accident last night.'

A spokesperson for Shelbourne Action, Doctor Ruby Watson,

said her group had been trying to alert authorities to the high levels of sulphur dioxide emissions from Hadron for some time.

Ruby's voice sounded calm and professional. '*We have evidence of emission rates double those accepted by the World Health Organization.*'

Hadron refused to comment on Doctor Watson's allegations.

When the newsreader moved onto the next story, Imogen switched the radio off.

'Holy shit,' she said. 'What about that?'

Hesse couldn't help but think of Jake's family. 'It's all happened so fast, hasn't it?'

'I can't believe it,' Imogen said, shaking her head. 'All those meetings, the market stalls, the letter-writing—we chipped away for five years with no result—and then in a couple of weeks, it suddenly takes off.'

Hesse thought about how scared Felicity had been the previous night. She must have known a big company like Hadron would find the most obvious scapegoat. And who better than the manager of a plant they wanted to offload anyway?

The supermarket car park was packed with media cars and vans when they arrived back in Shelbourne. There were half a dozen cameras set up on tripods on the footpath and people were being interviewed. Imogen took one look and drove straight past.

There was a scrum of cameras and reporters outside their house. The gate was closed and the formidable figure of Bear stood guard just inside. He saw Imogen approaching and signalled to her to keep driving and go in the back way. The property behind them was a holiday house Hesse often cut through to get to the main beach. Imogen drove around the block, turned into the empty driveway and parked.

When she and Hesse ducked through the tea trees into their own yard they found Oliver and Ruby sitting on the back deck. Ruby raised a bottle of champagne in one hand. 'We're hiding from the jackals,' she said, waving towards the front gate.

Hesse guessed it would look callous if they were caught celebrating the loss of eighty workers' livelihoods.

'Bear's keeping watch,' Imogen said. 'You'd better come inside and uncork that.'

The kitchen still smelled of breakfast. Ruby muted the popping of the champagne with a tea towel and poured three glasses. 'Hesse?' she asked.

'He's been the star of the campaign,' Oliver said.

Imogen relented. 'Just a small one.'

They clinked glasses. 'Here's to David taking down Goliath!' Oliver said.

'It's just a battle. We haven't won the war,' Ruby said. 'The closure may only be temporary.'

'True,' Oliver said. 'But with all the negative publicity Hadron is not going to find a buyer. And the shareholders are making a lot of noise about the company's reputation being trashed.'

Ruby checked herself. 'Oh, Hesse,' she said quickly. 'We're so sorry about Fenna. How is she?'

'Pretty knocked around. She'll be in hospital for a while,' he said.

Hesse's phone buzzed in his pocket. It was Felicity: *Can we talk?*

He stepped outside onto the back deck. *Sure*, he texted back.

Almost immediately his phone rang. 'Hey,' he said.

There was a long pause. He could hear her breathing.

'How's Fenna?' she asked. Her voice lacked its usual confidence.

Hesse told her about his visit to the hospital.

'She's going to be okay, though huh?'

'Yeah. But she's going home to the Netherlands.'

'I'm sorry,' she said. 'Everything's gone to shit, hasn't it?'

Hesse didn't answer.

'Are you still there?' she asked.

'Yeah, I'm here.' He guessed she hadn't rung just to talk about Fenna. 'What about you?' he asked.

She went quiet. He heard sniffing then a muffled sound like she was holding the phone against her chest. 'Dad's not good,' she said finally.

'Does he know you gave me the documents?'

'I don't know. He's not letting on if he does.'

'Why did you do it?' Hesse asked. 'You must have known he'd be blamed.'

Again, a long silence.

'Felicity?'

'I can't talk about it now,' she whispered.

'Are you'—he searched for the right word—'safe?'

'I've got to go,' she said.

19

Hesse visited Fenna in the hospital every day after school and then caught the late bus home. They made plans together while she slowly mended. Hesse promised to travel to the Netherlands as soon as he finished his year twelve.

A young female constable took Fenna's statement and seemed satisfied with her restrained answers. Colin Turner spent a lot of time at the hospital. He helped Fenna navigate all the formalities, the forms and statements the police and hospital needed before she could be discharged.

Jago's funeral was held at the Catholic church. Most of the town turned out and one of his mates from the footy club, Tom Gosper, a big man who looked uncomfortable in a suit, gave a stumbling eulogy. Hesse hardly recognised the Jago Crothers

Tom spoke about. Apparently he was kind and generous, a top guy who'd help out anyone in need. Hesse dug his fingernails into his palm as he thought about the Jago he knew, the one who'd kidnapped Fenna and nearly killed her.

No one at the funeral paid Hesse, Imogen or Bear any extra attention. For all they knew, it had been luck they'd arrived at the scene of the accident. And Imogen had done all she could for Jago until the paramedics had taken over.

Outside the church, the mourners milled about. Jago's mother, Beth, wept in the arms of her husband.

Bear brought his car around the front and Imogen and Hesse were walking towards it when Bob Crothers called to them.

Hesse froze.

Bob and Beth walked over to the car. 'We just wanted to say thanks,' Bob said, struggling to hold back tears. 'I know you did everything you could for our boy.'

Imogen gently leaned in and gave each of them a hug. 'We're so sorry for your loss,' she said.

'Did he…? Did he say anything, when, you know…?' Beth asked.

Imogen shook her head. 'I wish I could tell you something, Beth, but he wasn't conscious when we found him.'

She nodded, gathering herself again.

'And the girl?' Bob asked. 'How's she doing?'

'She'll be okay,' Hesse said. He wanted to tell them the truth, that she was broken and hurt and lost and it was all Jago's fault. But seeing their grief overwhelmed him. He shook Bob's hand and gave Beth a hug.

'That's good,' Bob said. He took Beth by the arm and led her back to the other mourners.

Hesse felt like he was sleepwalking through classes at school. One period drifted into another as he imagined himself sitting by Fenna's bed and holding her hand while they talked. The storm around the meeting and video subsided after a week or so and his friends stopped asking him about it. Jake was avoiding him. Hesse knew he blamed him for his father having been stood down at the mine.

Four days after the accident, Hesse met Fenna's parents at the hospital. Her father, Willem, was a tall, thin man with a shock of receding blond hair. He was quite formal, shaking Hesse's hand and nodding, but her mum, Eva, rushed at him and enveloped him in a hug. She kissed him three times on the cheeks then held him at arm's length to look at him.

'Hesse,' she said. 'Such a strange name for such a beautiful boy.'

'*Mama!*' Fenna said, cringing. 'You don't have to squeeze him to death.'

'But this boy, he saved you! In the car.'

'No,' Hesse said. 'I helped her.'

'Same thing,' Eva said. She was as tall as her husband, with red hair and a warm smile.

There were lots of questions, mostly from Willem, about the short time Fenna had spent in Shelbourne. Hesse was careful with what he told them, highlighting the surf lessons and the campaign against Hadron, but he couldn't avoid the accident.

Willem nodded at his answers without giving anything away. Eva, on the other hand, seemed to be looking for any opportunity to heap more praise on Hesse.

'Surfing! That's fantastic,' she enthused.

Fenna sunk further into her bed, eventually telling them she was tired and needed to rest. As they were leaving, she called Hesse back.

'Sorry about the interrogation,' she said. 'Dad's not always like that. He's just jetlagged.'

'And your mum?'

'No. She's *always* like that.'

A week later, Fenna went home to Shelbourne. Her parents would be staying with the Turners until they returned to the Netherlands with their daughter. Hesse spent as much time with her as he could manage. He wasn't sure whether Julie had told Willem and Eva she thought he and Fenna had been sleeping together.

There was a steady flow of visitors: Jake and Mus, together as always. Tina bustled in and out looking uncomfortable but wanting to show she cared, and Felicity sent flowers and a card.

Fenna's injuries made it hard for her to walk but she managed a slow lap of the block each day, her arm looped through Hesse's for support. It was the only way they could be alone, so they took their time, stopping in a quiet spot to hold each other and kiss. The swelling had eased around her eyes, but the bruises remained.

They knew their time was running out. The doctors had

given Fenna the okay to travel and the flights had been booked for the following weekend.

'I want to go to the beach one last time,' she said on Wednesday evening.

Hesse had no idea how they'd manage it, but he promised he'd make it happen. 'Friday after school,' he said. 'The weather's going to be okay.'

'Our last day,' Fenna said.

'For now,' Hesse interrupted. 'I told you I'm coming to the Netherlands when I finish year twelve.'

She looked at him like she wanted to believe him. 'Eighteen months is a long time,' she said, pulling him closer. 'Maybe you'll find another girlfriend, some surfer girl, and you'll forget all about me.'

'No chance,' he said, but even in the gathering gloom, he could see the sadness behind her smile.

It took a lot of convincing for Fenna's parents to allow the trip to the beach, but they relented when Imogen said she'd drive them. Hesse was right about the weather. It was one of those still, early winter evenings when it felt like the coast was clinging to the memory of warmer days. Imogen dropped them at the start of the track through the dunes, saying she'd be back in an hour to pick them up.

Hesse had been unsure about going to Corrals, but Fenna insisted.

'This is still our special place,' she said. 'It's where you taught me to surf.'

She struggled down the sandy track, but finally they made

it onto the beach. The ocean was like a mirror, catching the late afternoon light in the faces of the occasional waves. Hesse had brought a towel and he laid it in a protected hollow where the dunes met the beach. He sat with his legs wide and Fenna eased down with her back to him. He carefully wrapped his arms around her.

For a while they sat in silence, their bodies supporting each other. Hesse could feel the rise and fall of her breath, still labouring with the exertion of the walk. He inhaled the smell of her, trying to memorise it for the months to come when she'd be thousands of kilometres away. A small, perfectly formed wave rose from the ocean and peeled along the sandbank. He surfed it in his mind, pointing his imaginary board down the line and moving with the flow of it.

'What's going to happen with the power station?' Fenna asked.

'Who knows?' Hesse said. 'It's closed for now and no one seems to think it'll reopen anytime soon.'

'All because of you.'

'No,' he said. 'I was just a small part of it. It happened because of all the work people like Mum did for years, chipping away at Hadron. With your video and the documents from Felicity, it came together in a perfect storm. Oliver reckons they'll never find a buyer now.'

Fenna was quiet for a while. 'I'm going to get more active when I go home. This campaign has woken me up.'

'Me too. Closing one coalmine, one power station, it doesn't mean much in the scheme of things. We've gotta do more.'

'It's a start though.'

'Hey,' he said. 'We're running out of time. Let's talk about something else.'

She struggled to her knees and turned to face him. 'I'm going to miss you so much,' she said. 'I wish I could stay longer, for the whole term, like I was meant to. We could surf together. I could take you ice skating.'

'And teach me to dance?' he said.

'I'm not sure one term would be long enough for that,' she said.

Hesse looked at her, this girl who had appeared out of nowhere. The glow of the evening lit her face and highlighted the spray of freckles across the top of her nose. He tried to remember what he'd felt when he'd seen her that first time, sitting alone on the platform at Haystacks. In his head, he attempted to put everything in order: the moment she walked into the surf shop, the surfing lesson, the late night walks, the feeling of her hand slipping into his jacket pocket on the bus. How could a girl turn your life upside down so quickly?

'Come on,' she said. 'I want to feel the water one more time.' She undid her laces and slipped her shoes off. Hesse did the same.

He helped her up and they walked down the slope to the water. Fenna pulled the legs of her jeans up as far as she could and stepped into the shallows. She gave a little squeal. 'A girl could freeze her tits off in here,' she said.

Hesse laughed.

They waded in holding hands and stood looking out to the horizon.

20

It was early August before the biggest of the winter swells arrived, on a bitterly cold Saturday. Theo had closed for a month and headed north. Hesse had lain awake half the night listening to the dull roar of the waves fill the valley. He'd counted the intervals between booming sets and knew the swell was bigger than predicted. He dozed off and on until daybreak, then got up and made a quick breakfast. He'd been working up to this day for weeks, testing the board Theo had made for him in bigger and bigger waves until he was confident of handling Razors. But now the day had arrived, a cocktail of adrenaline and fear ate away at his confidence. As he shovelled Weet-Bix into his mouth he tried to distract himself by thinking of Fenna.

She'd been gone six weeks and he missed her every day, like

a part of him had been torn out and transported to the other side of the world. They spent hours on Skype each week but nothing could replace the little things that had made her real to him: the warmth of her skin, the unruly strands of her hair that had caught between their lips when they kissed, a single lifted eyebrow when she questioned him, the lilting sound of her voice.

Apart from the hole left by Fenna, Hesse's life in Shelbourne had settled back into the familiar groove of school, homework and surfing. The coalmine and power station had been closed permanently, and Hadron prosecuted for false reporting of emissions. The news cycle had moved on and the town was left to deal with the fallout. A few families had already left, and Bob Crothers had closed his workshop. Ibrahim had picked up some shifts at the supermarket, but his family's future in Shelbourne was uncertain. Jake no longer sat with Hesse on the bus and they had barely spoken since the closure. Meanwhile, the local clubs and organisations had banded together to lobby the government for special grants to keep them afloat until they found new sponsors.

Hesse and Rachel Cheng had become good friends and he'd joined the organising committee for the Castlereagh climate strike. It was huge. Schools had emptied and thousands of kids filled the streets, banging drums, singing and chanting, demanding to be heard. Hesse gave a speech on the steps of the town hall and *#I'mWithHesse* had trended again for a few hours. Rachel had fired up the crowd with chants and led them on the march. And Felicity had been right: with so many kids attending the strike, schools couldn't follow through on their threats of suspension.

Felicity hadn't returned to Castlereagh High. Her dad was transferred to another Hadron facility in South Australia while the EPA investigations continued. She'd disappeared from Hesse's life—no phone calls, no goodbyes—until he bumped into her at a party in Castlereagh at the end of July. She spied him across the room and smiled as she made her way towards him, a glass in her hand.

'Hesse,' she said above the noise of the room, leaning in to kiss him on the cheek.

He wasn't sure how to respond. 'Hey,' he said, eventually. 'What's happening?'

'Oh, you know, school, homework, party, repeat.'

'I heard you'd moved to South Australia,' he said.

She shook her head. 'My dad moved. Mum and I are in Castlereagh now.'

'Is that—?'

'Good? Yeah, it is.'

A tall boy who looked as though he'd spent a lot of time in the gym came up behind her and put his arm around her waist. 'Come on, babe,' he said. 'Let's dance.'

She smiled at him and took another sip of her drink. 'Gotta go,' she said to Hesse.

'Sure,' he replied. 'But, hey, thanks for helping with you-know-what.'

She leaned in close to his ear. 'We helped each other, Hesse.'

~

The house leaked heat overnight but it was still warmer than the air that hit Hesse when he walked out to the shed. He'd left a note for Imogen, rather than waking her. She'd worked a late shift and would probably sleep for another three hours yet. He also knew what her response would be if he told her he was going to surf Razors, so he just wrote: *Gone for a surf, back later.*

He loaded the new board onto the side rack of his bike and stuffed his wetsuit into the crate along with a dry towel and booties. He couldn't tell whether he was bracing himself against the cold or the fear that gripped him as he pushed the bike down the driveway and out onto the street. The wind had howled through the night but it had backed off a little now.

When Hesse hit Ocean Road he looked towards the surf shop. The windsock on the roof was horizontal in the offshore wind. He rounded the Fat Controller corner, where a couple of the early risers in the window seats gave him a wave, and began the climb up the hill past the surf club. When he reached the top, he pulled off the road at the lookout and gazed nervously towards Razors. Initially he was relieved. There were swell lines stacked to the horizon but they seemed to be passing through Razors without breaking. There was a solid right-hander peeling at the back of Wangim Point and inside the bay the sets were closing out the main beach. He thought maybe he'd misread the swell and it wasn't as big as it had sounded through the night. He was about to turn away when a massive bombie set reared up as it approached Razors. Hesse's heart jumped into his mouth. The wind caught the first wave and sent a huge plume of spray into the air as it exploded across the reef. The waves behind it were bigger still, breaking out on the furthest edge and engulfing the reef in white water.

Hesse's breath was coming fast as he saw the enormity of the challenge ahead of him. He couldn't see anyone else out—there were no black dots scraping over the top of the waves or dropping down the faces. Slowly, he wheeled his bike to the start of the track that led to the yacht club. This felt like the point of no return. Ignoring the voice in his head screaming at him to turn around, go home, get back into bed, he pushed off down the track towards the beach.

There were a dozen cars parked in the bays behind the yacht club. Some of them would be early-morning dog walkers, others non-surfers drawn to the beach by the roar of the swell. Hesse rode to the top of the concrete boat ramp and looked out towards Razors. It appeared calm now but he knew there would be a long break between sets.

A van pulled up beside him and the driver rolled down his window. It was Steve Daly.

'If it isn't the climate warrior,' he said with a smile.

Hesse shrugged. He hadn't seen Steve since the meeting.

Steve eyed the board in Hesse's rack. 'With a gun like that, I'm guessing you're not surfing the banks today,' he said.

'Nah, might head out the back of Wangim,' Hesse replied. 'Or…'

Steve nodded. 'Or Razors?'

'Maybe. What about you?'

Steve leaned on the steering wheel and peered through the

windscreen just as another set broke across the reef. 'It's big,' he said. 'Three metres on the sets, I reckon. You sure you can handle that?'

Hesse ran his palm along the rail of the board in the rack. 'I've got the stick for it,' he said.

'A Theo special?'

'Yeah.'

'Having the board for it and actually surfing Razors are two different things,' Steve said. His face softened as he looked at Hesse. 'But I'm going out and I wouldn't mind some company.'

Steve parked his van, and Hesse changed under the balcony of the yacht club. They took their time, stopping to look whenever a set hit. Two more carloads of surfers turned up but they drove further along towards Wangim Point. Steve and Hesse would have Razors to themselves.

The paddle out was long and tricky. The little bay in front of the yacht club was easy but once they got beyond the protection of the point they had to contend with a swift current sweeping them towards the main beach. Steve was quiet, sticking with Hesse, even though he was the stronger of the two. Hesse used the steady rhythm of the paddling to push down the fear and excitement that was building in his body. Everything looked different from when he had come out here on the big paddleboard a couple of months ago. He could barely make out the tower at the surf club, and the main beach was shrouded in spray from the close-out sets. They were still a hundred metres from Razors when they began to feel the rolling swell. It was too deep to break here but Hesse could feel the thickness and size of it, like some great beast was moving underneath him.

Steve had pulled ahead. Now he waited, sitting up on his board and watching the approach of the next set.

Hesse moved up next to him.

'This is the safe spot,' Steve said. 'If you get hit you'll be dragged across the reef, but eventually you'll be washed into deep water. Don't try to paddle back out through the right. Head this way and approach it from the same side every time.'

Hesse nodded but he only heard half of what Steve said. The first wave of a new set was approaching and it looked like a green-grey mountain looming up to swallow the sky. It seemed to feather for an age, growing steeper with every second until the weight of the lip was too much to hold aloft. They were sitting to the left of the peak and the wave broke right so they were barely able to see the face they were hoping to ride. On their side the wave shut down in a seething mass of white water. The spray lifted high in the air and rained down on them in the channel.

'See why you don't want to get too far inside?' Steve said, pointing. 'Stick to the right shoulder and only paddle in when you're sure you'll make it. I've been timing the sets. They're at about eight-minute intervals.'

Hesse couldn't speak. The wave was so much bigger and more threatening up close. When he'd seen it from the lookout the distance had made it appear manageable, but out here it was a completely different creature. And the sound it made—the deep percussive roar of water pounding onto the reef.

Steve was looking at him now. 'Having second thoughts?' he asked.

Hesse still couldn't find his voice.

'First time I came out here I was fifteen. I didn't get a wave,' Steve said. 'I made it look as though I was trying to get on them, but I wasn't really. I was shit-scared.'

Hesse nodded, knowing this man he hardly knew was telling him something deeply personal.

'What I'm saying is, you can paddle back in. No judgment,' Steve said.

Finally, Hesse found his voice. 'I'll wait here for a bit,' he said. 'Watch you.'

'Okay,' Steve said. 'You won't be able to just sit though. You'll drift. Keep paddling to hold your position.' He lay back down on his board. 'Wish me luck.'

Steve left Hesse in the channel and stroked confidently further out. It had been about three minutes since the last set so he had time to get into position. He disappeared behind each unbroken rolling swell, only to reappear at the top of the next one. A weak sun was doing its best to penetrate the cloud and thin beams reached Hesse where he sat on his board. Shivering had overtaken his body and he needed to move to get warm. He checked his position by looking back towards the yacht club then began to slowly paddle seaward, staying well clear of the reef.

When Steve came into view again he was sitting astride his board, his arms folded, his face turned to the horizon. As the next set approached, he pulled the board underneath him and paddled diagonally to where he anticipated the wave would break. Hesse watched from the safety of the channel as Steve stroked up the face of the first wave, flying off the back just as it started to feather. He disappeared in the trough between waves and when Hesse caught sight of him again, he'd swung his board around and was digging his arms into the water, paddling powerfully to get into position as the next one reared up behind him. He hovered on the lip before jumping to his feet, freefalling the first metre until the fins grabbed and he gained control. A less experienced surfer might panic and try to turn too quickly for the safety of the shoulder, but Steve waited until he was almost in the trough of the wave before he drew out a long bottom turn. To Hesse's eyes everything Steve did seemed to be in slow motion, at odds with the power and fury of what was happening around him.

Again, he waited until he was almost back to the top of the wave before he shifted his weight and carved a wide arc across the open face. He disappeared from view then and Hesse was left wondering if he'd made it to safety where the wave faded into deep water.

Five minutes passed before Hesse caught sight of Steve paddling towards him, a wide smile plastered across his face.

'What do you reckon?' he asked as he drew up next to Hesse. 'Want to have a crack?'

Hesse didn't know whether watching Steve had made him more confident or more afraid. He'd seen how it could be done but didn't know whether he had the skill—or the courage—to do it himself. Despite the sickening feeling that had taken over his body, the jangling nerves and the buzzing in his ears, he found himself nodding.

'Stick with me,' Steve said. He moved off quickly, taking away any opportunity for Hesse to change his mind.

Hesse laid his hand on the deck of the board and, for a moment, thought about his dad. Then he dug in with strong, deep strokes and followed Steve. They were still in the channel when the next set hit, allowing Hesse to pinpoint the position he'd need to be in to take off.

There were six waves in the set, and when it had passed, the ocean resumed an eerie calm. Hesse and Steve took the opportunity to paddle through the impact zone, and get to the other side, where the right shoulder would give them access to the peak. Hesse sat a little wider than Steve, eyeing the distant surf club tower to orientate himself. Steve either hid his fear more successfully than Hesse, or he didn't have any. He was focused but still seemed to be enjoying the experience.

'When you get the chance, you have to go,' Steve said without taking his eyes off the horizon. 'Don't hesitate on the lip, you've gotta commit.'

'Okay,' Hesse said.

The next set was probably the same size as the ones Hesse had already watched barrel over the reef, but from this new position it seemed bigger still. He dug in and followed Steve as they headed further out and across towards the first wave. It reared up out of deep water faster than Hesse anticipated and he had to scratch over the top to save himself from being driven into the reef. The second wave was bigger again. As Hesse scrambled for the shoulder, Steve paddled directly towards the peak, pivoted his board just as the wave started to feather and put in half a dozen deep strokes. He jumped to his feet and was lost from Hesse's view as he pointed his board down the face.

Hesse had never felt more alone but there was no time to dwell on it. The next wave blanked out the horizon. For now, it was everything in his world. And it was coming directly towards him, its face like a massive mouth opening to swallow him up. He should have felt terror at the prospect of being hit and held down, ragdolled across the reef. The adrenaline was still mainlining through his body and his heart was working double overtime, but something else was wrestling for control. All those years of surfing the banks and smaller points had led to this moment. Maybe everything that happened with Fenna, the campaign and Jago too. He turned his back to the wave and paddled as hard as he could until he felt it pick him up, its power propelling him forward. From the top of the mountain he looked into the dark pit in front of him and hesitated for an instant. He may have closed his eyes, or maybe it was the spray that blinded him. But he leaped to his feet and felt the immediate weightlessness of the little freefall before his fins connected with the wave again. It was so much steeper than anything he'd ever surfed and his first instinct was to try to get to safety out on the shoulder. But he remembered Steve's first wave, the way he'd waited and waited before drawing out his bottom turn. Hesse held his nerve for as long as he could before he leaned into the face, being careful not to dig the rail too deep. He had no time to appreciate the artistry in the board Theo had shaped for him, the way it had been made specifically for this wave, but it gave him an advantage when he swooped into that turn and generated speed off the bottom. He flew out onto the wall, staying ahead of the surge as the wave steepened again. Below him he could see the shadow of the reef, shallower than he could ever have imagined. Hesse dared a couple of small movements up and down the face but there was no time for artful cutbacks or graceful flicks off the lip, just a straight line to survival.

Then it was over. The wave lost speed as it hit deep water and Hesse eased his way over its shoulder. Even as he slowed his feet remained anchored on the board and it wasn't until then that a primal scream erupted from his lungs.

Twenty metres ahead, Steve sat in the channel with both arms in the air, the universal surfers' salute of respect.

Hesse dived off, feeling the tug of his legrope before surfacing and daring to breathe again. He had no words for what he'd just done.

Steve paddled up to him. 'Not bad,' he said, smiling. 'You should have a go at a big one next time.'

Hesse felt the release of all the tension that had been dammed up inside him, the uncoiling of tendons in his neck and shoulders. He laughed.

'Want to go again?' Steve asked.

'Why not?' Hesse replied.

As Steve paddled away from him, Hesse looked back towards town. The sky had cleared and the windows of the surf club tower caught the morning sun. Below it, he knew Skegs would have planted the BEACH CLOSED signs firmly in the sand above the high-tide mark. Up the top of Russell Street his mum would be sleeping in their little leaning house, the prayer flags flapping their prayers in the wind and the moonah branches rubbing against the spouting. Past the ridge, the power station rusted in the salt air. And thousands of kilometres beyond Shelbourne, on the other side of the world, a girl with a spray of freckles across her nose would be yawning and getting ready for bed. And maybe she'd be thinking of a boy thousands of kilometres away, on the other side of the world, who couldn't dance but who she'd fallen for anyway.

'Oi,' Steve called. 'You coming?'

Hesse didn't answer. The adrenaline was kicking in again and he put it to good use, paddling strongly back out to sea.

ACKNOWLEDGMENTS

Many people have helped bring this book to fruition.

First, thank you to Marieke Jacobi and Anne Hofstra for educating me in all things Dutch and for generously offering so much detail about your experiences of Australia. Fenna is neither of you but there are parts of both of you in her. Thank you for your early readings of the manuscript and for correcting my rudimentary Dutch.

To Nicole Maher for once again reading raw drafts and pointing me in the right direction. Your support over the last six years has been unwavering. Great Escape Books is a haven for readers and writers and a literary hub on the west coast.

To Gail Chrisfield for your intuitive beta reading of the manuscript. I hope I have done your insights and experience justice in the finished text.

To my in-family first readers, Lynne, Harley and Bella—thanks for being the guinea pigs and for being so positive.

To everyone at Text, especially my editor, Jane Pearson, for once again highlighting the blind spots and for believing in the story from day one. Thanks also to the whole team who have put their considerable skills behind getting this book out into the world: Jamila Khodja, Emily Booth, Kate Lloyd, Stef Italia and Julia Kathro. Thanks to Design by Committee for the stunning cover and to Michael Heyward for continuing to believe in and support Australian writing.

Thanks to the Class of 2016, to Shyama Buttonshaw for the board information and Louis Sisk for the medical and surgical details.

A big shout out to the Shut It Down crew. Our campaign achieved something remarkable and was the inspiration for the writing of this book—in which all characters are fictitious and bear no resemblance to anyone living or dead!

And finally, to my family, Lynne, Oliver (who finally gets a gig), Maddy, Harley and Bella. Thank you for your support, your not-so-gentle ribbing and your love.